"OH LYDIA, OH LYDIA, my darling encyclopedia here we go! And coming around the final bend—what? Who's this in the lead? Jerry Jackson! Impossible! He's a ten-thousand-to-one shot. And look at his jockey, folks, Lydia the Encyclopedia. She's pounding the hell out of that poor old nag. Jerry doesn't seem to care. He acts like he either loves a good pounding or is damn well used to it.

"He's trying like hell to please her! He's giving it all he can—which isn't much—but it's everything. The whip means nothing to him. Pleasing Lydia is everything. Could he win, folks? Could the impossible come true? Could he be another Trump?

"They're coming around the final lap, folks. Jerry's taking the lead. Could it be? Could it be? Oh, my God, I think he might win, folks. Unbelievable! Incredible! The impossible is going to be done. Ten thousand to one! Hooray to those dumb assholes who picked Jerry! Who would ever buy a ticket on him?

"Oh, my darling encyclopedia! We are going to win tonight, I feel it, and you will make it so. You are my secret. You will make me win whether I want to or not. You're the best jockey in the world."

JERRY JACKSON STOOD ALONE by his darkened window. He glanced at his wristwatch. It was seven minutes before seven. He would go downstairs at seven—not six fifty-nine or seven-o-one. He was a short guy, probably five-five or five-six with a strong build. He could have done well at golf or tennis in his younger days. He was outfitted in fancy cowboy attire fit for a barbeque or watching a rodeo. His shirt was tan with fancy dark brown leather patches. It was tucked neatly into his blue jeans which in turn were tucked into his short leather riding boots.

His bedroom, on the second floor, was purposefully dark so he could watch all below and remain invisible. His butler, Oliver, was directing the parking to different areas of the massive lawn. As each person or couple emerged, Jerry made mental evaluations and then passed them on to Lydia as if she were standing beside him.

"Not much longer, my dear Encyclopedia, before the fun begins.

"Oh my! Here comes Dolph and his pack. I swear that guy puts on a pound a day. If he were pregnant, he'd deliver a litter. Hell, if he fell on his stomach, I wonder if his arms would touch the ground. Now, Lydia, my dear, he's betting big bucks on me to win. He wants me gone. He wants my job. Then, you know what would happen? He'd put on ten pounds a day. He'd blow up like a balloon in two months. Maybe that's why his gang of three stay with him. Sure, that must be it. But who of the three would replace him?

"Let's see, Lydia dear—who would the guys who bought us out appoint if Dolph Briskie died? Angela Cushing? I doubt it. She's just been a secretary all her life. But then again, she's a gal. They'd gain points putting her on top. Ray Butler, the company manager? Good chance. He's big. He's powerful. And he's black. They'd gain points with him, too. Probably the best guy for the position would be John Peter Shielding, company accountant. He knows every detail of everything that's going on, but gees, Lydia, he's great on numbers but a minus on people. I think he'd be happiest if everything were machines and people did not exist. He's ice cold. Could all three become joint managers? Whatever, Dolph and his gang of three sure as hell want me to win and be gone. I hope to please them.

"Oh my, my darling Encyclopedia, look who's coming now—Jules and his lovely wife, Hilda. He's the child we never had. A drug peddler! Eh, he probably would have been great at that, too. As you know, Hilda converted him.

"She wouldn't date a drug peddler. I told you about the day he came to me on the fire trail. Reluctantly, I gave him a job because we nodded every day when he took his every morning run past me and Moresee, my fabulous Airedale. I had my doubts. No more. Now he's our best. He's the top of the ladder. Lucky us. Lucky him. Lucky Hilda. It's worked out great for all of us.

ACCIDENT

SUICIDE

or

MURDER

a novel by

DAN MAHL

"He's become a big company asset. I didn't do it. It was beautiful Hilda. He fell for her and tossed drug business to get her, I don't blame him—no, no Lydia, dear Lydia there's nothing between me and Hilda. She's all Jules and vice versa. But to get her, he had to stop the drug peddling and get an honest job. We gave him one. Now they're married with a child on the way—cement. Yeah, he's cost us a lot, but the money spent is cheap in comparison. He's been great for me and the company. He's the son and she's the daughter we never had. I'm proud of both of them. If you could meet them, you'd feel the same. I'm sure of it. No doubt about it—they're rooting for me. They want me to win—not to get rid of me, but because it's what I want.

"And coming around the corner of the house, folks, is playboy brother, Paul, with his gal of the week or day. Sure, he can get her drunk for free on our money. Oh, wait, my darling encyclopedia, I think that's Senator Hazelton. Is he worried? Good! I hope he has a good reason to be.

"Oh my, here's the damn fire trail Ranger who cost us three hundred fifty bucks because Moresee pooped in the woods. It took us fifteen or twenty minutes to find it and take it out of the grass where it would have been fertilizer, food for plants and insects. Instead, we had to wrap it in a plastic bag where it became just plain shit.

"Oh yes, some of the neighbors are here out of curiosity and there is the gang of assassins who work for different papers but they all think the same—destroy all who don't think the same as they do. They are always right and everyone else is always wrong. They're blind to the truth.

"What the hell is this?" Jerry forgot talking to Lydia. "How did they find out about tonight? Three black Muslims all in white flowing robes and correct Muslim headgear. Two are giants and the other normal size. He must be the boss with his protection. Somethings wrong here. Should I change things?"

J. J. stepped away from the window for a moment. He shook his head firmly. "Hell no! They want to hear what I'm going to say—good! They'll hear it."

"OK Lydia. It's time to start. I think the deck is stacked against us. Put the whip to me. I'll run as fast as I can."

He glanced at his wristwatch. It was one minute before seven. He glanced one last time out the window. Eleven cars covered his lawn. That was twenty-two of the good guys. Good! He'd need them. The TV crew had come hours earlier and J. J. had enjoyed trying to help their set-up even if they, too, were probably assassins.

Two newspaper assassins had arrived thirteen minutes ago and they were standing outside waiting for one or more to arrive. J. J. recognized one assassin being from the local newspaper and the other probably from a national paper. The assassins loved to kill and destroy. All must think like they do. Freedom of thought must die.

Moresee, his faithful Airedale, watched every move J. J. made. He sensed something was wrong, and was hoping he'd find out soon.

J. J. sighed a good-bye to Lydia and left the bedroom. Moresee followed, and they crossed to the center of the mezzanine that overlooked the foyer.

The staircase wound slowly to the white and black marble floor of the foyer. In the middle of the foyer was a large bowl of assorted flowers on a round oak table which was covered with a colorful Persian mat. Beneath the table was a large matching Persian rug.

J. J. hurried down the winding staircase using the bannister, which was chest high, for balance. Moresee followed closely behind and was panting with concern. Each spoke of the bannister was a realistic carving of a fish or small animal. The closed double doors to the living room could not contain the happy and congenial party noise from within.

J. J. opened the door. Moresee squeezed tightly beside him to avoid being excluded. The room became silent for a brief moment and then exploded in cheers. J. J.'s eyes glanced at the assassins. They had expectant slight smiles of their faces. This was going to be fun.

Each of the guests had wine or a cocktail in one hand and either prawns, chicken wings, caviar, or another appetizer in the other. They were having a grand time and made sure J. J. knew their appreciation. J. J. advanced through the happy throng with handshakes and pats on his back. Moresee was invisible to the group and had to weave around and through legs to keep pace.

J. J. got to the huge fireplace at the far end of the room with three fresh unburned logs in it, and stood on the hearth which was about two feet higher than the floor. Happy Moresee lay down in front. The room became silent and waited.

"Thank you for coming, one and all. I hope you're enjoying your drinks and snacks."

Cheers of approval flooded the room.

"As you know, but maybe you don't so I'll tell you. Our company was recently accepted by the stock market. Now we have been bought by a large company. As a result, I'm about three hundred and fifty million bucks richer. Not as good as some of the high-tech companies, but damn good enough for me.

A few applauded.

"OK, now I have a ton of money. What the hell am I going to do with it?

"Retire? Take trips? Give parties? Start a new business? Give me a break! I'm seventy-two. I now have money falling out of my pockets and don't want to do any of that. Then I decided I wanted the best of everything." He looked at Dolph who looked worried.

"I went to the nearest nursery and asked for the owner or manager. When he came out, I told him…

I want the best tree you have and I'll pay up to a million dollars for it.

"The best tree, sir? They are all different. There is no best. What do you want to do with it?"

"I want to put it in the middle of my lawn. I want the best."

"I'm sorry, sir. I can't help you. There is no best tree. They are all different. Tell me, sir, what is your preference?"

"Then it hit me—difference—preference. That is true of all. There is no best. Each person thinks differently and so the best to one may not be the best to another. Everything is different. There is no best. It is individual opinion or preference. There is no best tree, person, race, or anything else, It is your preference or individual opinion.

"I'm telling you what I think is true. If the public accepts my thoughts, I'll step aside and Dolph will take my place and position."

Dolph's faced relaxed into a smile. J. J. paused and the room stayed mostly silent—a few soft claps.

"I decided to run for Senate of the United States from our great state of California. I want to be a button on President Trump's jacket.

The room remained silent. Dolph looked greatly concerned.

"When I was twelve, sixty years ago, a discriminating person was an admired guy. He was bright—intelligent. He knew right from wrong. He knew that one should not use a fork or knife to consume soup. One should use a spoon or specifically a spoon designed for soup—what's called a soup spoon. A person who refuses to discriminate will continue the futile effort of using his knife or fork to consume his soup. Their contention is that a spoon is not superior to a knife or fork. They are all equal. If you chose to use a spoon over the knife or fork, you are a knife and fork bigot—equality must rule. Knives, forks, and spoons are all equal. Sounds pretty damn dumb, doesn't it? You're right it is."

The room was now becoming restless and people were exchanging worried glances. Some were looking almost ill.

"So if you are a knife and fork bigot, you are to be shunned. You are a social outcast. You are ignorant. You are mean and I can't think of all the other rotten words you are.

"Actually, you are intelligent. You have made an intelligent choice. Let the ignorant people consume their soup with knives and forks. Differences are beautiful and wonderful. We shouldn't act as if being different is in any way an insult. It's wonderful.

"Each person in this room is different from everyone else here and in the rest of the world. Each of us is unique. Some are better at numbers, some are better at words, some are athletes, and some are mechanics or a million different abilities. Differences go on forever. We are all different. Our whole world is made of differences which is wonderful?

"Now here comes the shocker. I say the races are different. The white race is lazy, miserable, and loaded with complainers. The black race makes contentment and happiness wherever they are."

Again shocked, embarrassed silence.

"Here's a quick picture for you. Go into a black church that's in session. What greets you? Singing and dancing by the whole congregation. They're having a great time—it's fun, it's a blast. The music is full of life and so is the entire congregation. Now get in your car and drive to a white church in session. It's silent. People can only whisper. There's the moaning voice of the priest speaking in a language you don't even understand. Maybe there's a distant solemn organ or some glum moaning of a hymn, but the entire congregation is silent. It's like a funeral. It's glum. It's morose.

"The blacks are having a great time singing and dancing. They're happy. The white congregation is silent as if in a chamber or horror. As the priest talks, many in the congregation fall asleep. They don't understand a word he's saying.

"Just look at white history. white guys used to walk across the yard to the outhouse. They'd bitch and moan. They'd get wet when it rains, frozen when it snows, and sweat like hell in the hot summer. Then a miracle. Some lazy white guy finally had enough and built a toilet that could be used in the house. Then another lazy white guy got tired of washing, feeding, and cleaning up after horses and cars were built. The white guys complained cars weren't fast enough so airplanes were built. Some lazy white guy got sick and tired of having to walk across the street to talk to his neighbor. Bingo! The telephone. I guess you see the picture. Too lazy to wash dishes—dishwashers. Too lazy to sweep floors—vacuums, and on and on it goes. More machines to do the work for the lazy white race; so more factories needed to be built for them to escape having to work.

"Now some white guys have extra time and need something restful like music. So the lazy white guys invented musical instruments and then symphonies bloomed to create beautiful, restful sound.

"Look at the results of all this laziness. Instead of beautiful forests and fields, we have cement roads, cities crowded with houses, factories, theaters, symphonic halls, sport centers and on and on. Our laziness has destroyed the beauty of nature. We call the destruction we've created civilization ."

No one had taken a sip of anything. The wine was aging in their hands. Some appetizers were about to fall on the floor. It was impossible to believe what they were hearing.

"Now they're two different groups in the black race. There is the black American who is one of us. Then there are the African Americans who have the happy African inside them but also have the bitching complaining American part.

"How much would you complain if you made millions of dollars a year and only had to work six or so months? Pretty good deal, don't you think? We have some African American athletes who make millions in less than a year's work and won't stand for our two-minute-long national anthem. There is no other country in the entire world where they could do as well. Instead of spitting in the face of America, they should be kissing the American ground in thanks."

All those who were standing had to find a chair.

"Now we come to our previous president, Obama, who is half white and half black. His confusion is obvious. We know his white half is lazy. If he had a problem, he'd go play golf. It is his black half that is a mystery. Did he want to build and improve our country, or did he want to convert America to Africa? If he is black American, he will work to improve us in every possible way. If he is African American, he will find fault with all America has done in the past and criticize our great history because Africa is his model. I think he made it clear—he was our African-American president.

"When Obama was president, he was the most dangerous man in America. Why? He wanted to be the first dictator of America. Who is now the most dangerous man in America? Obama. He wants to replace 'of the people, by the people, and for the people' to 'of the politicians, by the politicians, and for the politicians.' He doesn't want to restore America. He wants to destroy America.

"There are basically three types of people and religions—builders, followers, and destroyers. A small percent are builders and destroyers. Let's look at what Christianity has built—football, baseball, basketball many more sports. Christianity has created novels and plays, musical instruments, symphonies, the internet, cars, trains, airplanes, skyscrapers, and thousands more. Finally, under what religion was our civilization born? Christianity. Christianity is a building religion. The followers are peaceful. Most religions are peaceful, including the Muslim religion, perhaps the largest religion in the world with approximately one and a half billion devotees.

"However, they do have a loud destroyer faction. Perhaps it's only ten percent or one hundred and fifty million destroyers—half the population of the United States, but if there's twenty percent destroyers, that's roughly our entire population. Keep your eyes and minds open. Be careful!

"What does all this have to do with voting for me? Simple—stop being brainwashed. Stop being afraid of seeing, thinking, and telling the truth. Scientists think they know all. They don't. They think God is a myth. He isn't. By the way, I'm a delighted 'follower' of Christianity. I hope all of you are, too.

"OK. Let's get onto something downright funny—gay weddings. Pete is going to marry Joe and start a family and raise the offspring to be upstanding citizens. Liz and Jane decide to do the same thing. But wait a minute, folks—they cannot produce children. They can't? Are you sure? Positive. They can't produce children? Nope. Then how can it be called a marriage? The reason for marriage is to renew human life. If same-sex unions cannot produce life, they are not married. The whole thing is a joke, a sham, a mockery of the reason for marriage. We have less than two percent of our population wanting to change what the original and true meaning of marriage is to a fantasy marriage.

Some of his friends wanted to leave, but didn't.

"Lets change the subject and talk about something soothing and relaxing like music. Remember the good old songs like 'Tea for Two' and 'Oh What a Beautiful Morning'? I'd hear one of those songs once and the melody would stick with me all day or maybe all week long. 'Day would break and I'd awake to find you'd baked a sugar cake for me to take for all the boys to see' or 'Oh what a beautiful morning, oh what a beautiful day. I have a wonderful feeling everything's going my way.'"

"Most of the music today is noise without melody. The lyrics aren't sung. They're chanted or shouted, and they go something like this, 'Hey bitch, kiss my ass, and don't bitch about the gas.' Musical instruments—not needed. All you need are the jungle drums. Hey, hey jungle. Here we come! And maybe we are returning to the jungle.

"Let's try this. Most of our current laws have become another form of taxation. The cities, counties, states, and our federal government need any and all the money they can get. They are all bankrupt and think that printing tons of unbacked dollars can solve the problem. It's a dangerously expanding bubble. It's going to explode, and the explosion will be heard around the world.

"Most of the agencies that were designed to serve us have been converted to tax collectors. They are looking for you to make a mistake, any mistake, so they can reap the praise and rewards of taking some of your money.

"You probably think I'm finished. I'm not. This is the most important thing I have to say. The scientists are also lying to us. Global warming is a lie. That the Universe started with an accidental 'Big Bang' is a bigger lie based on their initial premise that God does not exist. That is a lie.

"Accidents cannot be consistent. Accidents do not repeat themselves consistently. It is virtually impossible, and yet they claim our origins are an accident. It's a lie.

"When my good man Oliver wakened me this morning at six-thirty, I looked out the window and said with amazement, "Oliver, look at that! The sun is rising in the East this morning."

"Yes, sir. It is."

"Isn't that amazing?"

"Not really, sir. It does so every morning."

"Not every morning, Oliver. Didn't it rise from the North yesterday?"

"I'm afraid not, sir."

"You mean this whole week it has risen in the East?"

"This whole week and forever, sir."

"Forever! How can that be?"

"It just is, sir. The sun always rises in the East, makes a loop over us, and sets in the West. It has done so every day forever. It is consistent, sir."

"How can that be when our Universe and everything was created by a huge Big Bang accident?"

Oliver just nodded, smiled, and left.

"Then I thought about it. Accidents have zero consistency. The word means an unexpected event that is not expected to repeat. Yet the sun rises every morning in the East and sets in the West. It is one hundred percent consistent. Now look at the rest of our Universe. Without any friction or atmosphere all our stars, planets, and moons are round. None are randomly shaped pieces as if from a giant explosion. How many round pieces have you found after a dynamite blast? If you find one, it's an accident. Our Universe is consistent. All major bodies are consistently round.

"All the germs, insects, flowers, trees, animals, fish consistently reproduce their own kind consistently. If you plant corn, only corn will grow one hundred percent of the time. It is consistent.

"Each of us is consistently the same. Our heart, our arms and legs, our head, our shoulders, our internal parts are consistently the same on all of us.

"Doctors rely on our internal parts being where they should be, and they are. They are there consistently one hundred percent of the time.

"Our Universe can be explained mathematically as Einstein proved, but how can anything be explained mathematically that is not consistent? Since we are surrounded by consistency, then it is not accidental because accidents have ZERO consistency. If it is not accidental, then it has been designed. If so, then there is a designer. We call that designer God.

"And how about evolution? We are told it takes thousands of years for evolution to produce new forms of life. Well folks, we've had millions of years. Evolution should be in full bloom. Where are the new lions, and tigers, and bears oh my? What has replaced the oak, maple, and pear trees? After millions of years evolution should be in full swing. There should be all kinds of new things popping up all around us. There ain't. Instead of myriads of new species, we're fighting like mad to prevent the species we still have from extinction. Why hasn't the worm evolved into something else? Evolution is scientific brainwashing.

"Now look at how smart the guys you elected are to run our state. Last year we had a drought. This year we have floods. We're in constant trouble. Well. If that's true for all these years, why haven't they solved the problem? It's simple—build desalination plants up and down the entire coast of California. Our entire coast is alongside the Pacific Ocean. Give the desalinized water to the farmers and the mountain water to the people. Droughts and floods would never be problems.

"The dry weather would be enjoyed. Why haven't they put in these plants? Simple. They don't want us to be free. They look at us as if we were a herd of dumb, stinking skunks. They want us fenced in and under their control so we can't see what they're doing and stink up the place.

"Our current city, state, and federal governments want everyone to be the same—no differences. I want people to think and act as different individuals. I will support the builders and fight the destroyers. President Donald Trump wants to strengthen and improve the structure of our country, the welfare of our citizens, and our military and on and on. He is a builder. All those that oppose and are trying to ruin him whether in his own party or another are destroyers. They are bad, evil and they are the ones who should be destroyed.

"Their main objection to President Trump is his wanting the citizens of the United States to run the country. They want full control. They want to be god, king, emperor, dictator or whatever. The citizens of the USA are to be their slaves. They need to destroy President Trump. If you vote for me, I will support the builders in this country and the world. Let's all support the builders and improve us and all around us and let the destroyers muddle in their mud.

"To fix all the bad laws passed by Congress, only one thing needs to be done. Make it that all laws they pass applies to everyone including all the members of Congress, the Senate, Supreme Court, and our president—everyone. All laws passed apply to EVERYONE especially those who made and passed them.

"If Obama care had applied to all those who passed it, including Obama, it never would have passed. It is a rotten law. Since Obama care did not apply to them—it passed and we're stuck with it. That's about it, folks. You know what I think and believe. Vote for me or not. It's in your hands. Good-night all."

Jules and Hilda applauded with loud enthusiasm. J. J. smiled and nodded to them, then closed his eyes. "Well, Lydia my darling encyclopedia, I guess I flunked. Two are with me—dear Jules and Hilda. All the others just wanted to get the hell out. Dolph will be upset. He's been anxiously waiting to have me gone." He opened his eyes but kept talking to her. "Oh, my dear Lydia, I want to find out about Jules and his Muslim friends, but here comes Dolph. The problems are about to start. I hope you can watch."

His eyes glued on the three Muslims beside Jules and Hilda. They didn't look happy. Dolph and his gang were trying to cross through the exiting crowd.

The room emptied silently. The three assassins slunk outside to a secluded spot.

"Holy shit!" Gil Evers of the local paper shook his head. "What the hell are we going to do with all that shit?"

Harvey Menders smiled. "That's the wonderful thing. We don't do a damn thing. He just committed suicide. Did you hear the great applause when he

finished? Two only. J. J. is finished. We make his speech headlines and print every damn word. He's a dead man."

Joe Beister smiled. "You're right Harv. Let's do it!"

They left in the best possible mood. Gil even laughed aloud on his drive home.

CONVERSATIONS

J. J. STARTED TO WALK to Jules and Hilda. Dolph charged through those leaving as if he were carrying a football. He left his blockers straggling behind and won without them.

J. J. shouted to Jules, "Don't leave. I want to talk to you and meet your friends."

Jules nodded agreement and took the apparent leader of the Muslim contingency by his arm with his left hand, Hilda walked closely by his right side, and they headed toward J. J.

"That was really good, J. J. You fooled your small group here." Dolph shook his head with an attempt to smile. His gang slowly formed behind him. "I'll get tons of people in a big stadium to really start your campaign."

"In what way? I just started it." J. J. shook his head and turned to Jules, "Who are your friends?"

"This is Charlie. I've told you about him many times."

"Glad to finally meet you, Charlie, and your two friends. Jules never told me you were Muslim." J. J. stuck his hand out to Charlie who hesitated but shook it. J. J. then offered his hand to the other two. Charlie pushed J. J.'s hand aside.

"They're not social," Charlie explained. "They're just my bodyguards."

"You sure had me fooled, J. J.," Dolph persisted. "I took you seriously. I thought you were really going to run for Senator. I guess it was all a joke."

"I'm glad you enjoyed it," J. J. replied. He turned to Charlie. "How long have you been a Muslim?"

"Just a couple months," Charlie replied and watched J. J. "Why?"

"It caught me by surprise."

"Does that make a difference to you?" Charlie challenged as if ready to attack.

"I don't give a damn what religion you are. This is America. You're free to choose. What religion were you before?"

"None."

"Just out of curiosity, why did you decide to become a Muslim?"

"I think you have something against Muslims."

"Not at all—just curious. Maybe it's something I should do also."

"That was a great joke," Dolph persisted.

"No need for you," Charlie replied. "Under Obama, I was invisible. Things might be different now."

"Interesting," JJ nodded. "And if so, what will you change to now? What will make you invisible now?"

Charlie waited for a moment and studied J. J.'s face which was about a foot below his. He could wipe the floor with this old fart, but Jules would never allow that. "I've got nothing to return to. I'm happy the way it is. No changes."

"What's so damn funny?" J. J. turned to Dolph.

"I thought you were running for Senator, not Priest or Pastor." Dolph's fat, flabby cheeks shook like jelly as he laughed. Angela, on his right side, sort of smiled as backing. Powerful Ray by his left, watched J. J. closely. Fighting was fun and J. J. was so small he'd be able to throw him anywhere he wanted or bounce him like a basketball. J. P. Shielding was on his cell phone lingering behind.

"He's right," Jules stepped in. "You completely skipped over the biggest group in our country as if you hated them."

Dolph smiled. He was getting support from J. J.'s biggest supporter. J. J. narrowed his eyes.

"What group is that?" J. J. asked.

"The cell phone group—like Shielding's using right now. They're blind and deaf to all that's happening around them."

All eyes turned to Shielding who put his phone in his pocket with a curious frown. What had he done? Why were they all looking at him?

J. J. smiled and Jules continued. "What you said would only be understood by old, decrepit people who remember what made America strong. You need to get the young, active group that live on their phones. You skipped right over them. You ignored them completely. You dumped them. That was mean and rude. How could you possibly expect to win? Dolph is right. Hardly anyone believes in God today. It's almost an embarrassment, but looking into your cell phone is considered normal. People's phones are now their Gods."

J. J. chuckled. This was fun.

"Are you making a joke of what I said?" Dolph puffed up and took a step toward Jules.

"Not at all, Dolph." Jules looked at Dolph and smiled kindly. Hilda held onto his right arm as support. "Your observations were interesting. Unfortunately, there are no cell phone priests."

"Of course not!" Dolph was confused and looked at J. J. who nodded to him with an understanding smile. Dolph had intended to put J. J. down. Now he was being put down. He turned to Jules with almost a snarl, nodded to him and said nothing.

"What do you think I should have said?" J. J. asked Dolph.

Dolph turned back to J. J. and tried to make a pleasant face. "Well, J. J., after listening to what you said, I can't figure out who would want to vote for you. You seemed to attack everyone. Who are you trying to appeal to?"

"All those Americans who have no fear of the truth. All those who are not hiding behind social correctness. All those who can see how we're slipping down into the mud and drowning. It's an ugly death with mud in our teeth and lungs. OK, people are living now on their cell phones. What will they do and where will they turn if electricity is turned off one way or another? Their cell phone gods will be dead. Our current science teachings start with the premise that God does not and never has existed. Consistency proves they are wrong."

"It's not that big a group is all I was trying to point out." Dolph was trying to back out gracefully.

"The worst thing for you would be," Jules added, "if J. J. were not elected and resumed his position of running our company."

"Damn!" Dolph exploded. "Do you think I'm saying all this for self-interest?"

Jules shrugged and smiled.

Dolph turned to J. J. "You certainly don't think that, do you?"

"Of course not my old pal." J. J. patted Dolph on the shoulder. "We built the company with my money and your salesmanship. We've always been a good team." To change the subject, J. J. turned to Charlie, "Would you vote for me?"

"I don't vote. Never have—never will."

"How about your Muslim friends?"

"Got none."

"Interesting." J. J. nodded and pondered."And Hilda, what did you think of all I said?"

"I liked it. I thought it was new, refreshing and interesting. I had problems, however, with the fork, knife, and spoon part. I didn't quite understand it."

"It was to show that discrimination is not terrible—it is good. Let's say you sit down at a table to eat. In front of you is a knife, fork, and spoon. A cup of soup is brought. A discriminating person would see the soup could be consumed best with a spoon. Then a beef steak was brought. A discriminating person would choose a knife to cut it. When cut, he would take the fork to spear the pieces and put them in his mouth. If you don't discriminate, you say 'a spoon is just as good as a knife' and try to cut your steak with the spoon and drink your soup with a fork or knife. Everyone would call you stupid. If you don't discriminate and see even minute differences, you are blind. Everything is different. It is up to us to see, appreciate, and applaud those wonderful differences. Discrimination is important and good."

"Thank you, J. J." Hilda nodded and smiled.

"OK," J. J. said. "Let's get the hell out of here. See you on the fire trail tomorrow," he nodded at Jules, "and you in the office later," he nodded to Dolph, "and you," he nodded to Charlie, "who knows?"

'Hey, hey!" A voice shouted from the double doors. They all turned to see a powerfully built white guy. "What's going on? Where's everyone going? Has it all been called off?"

"It's over, Alex." Jules shook his head with a slight smile. "Where the hell have you been?"

"I thought it started at nine." Alex's voice dropped low.

"Seven, Alex, I told you seven." Jules shook his head.

"I must have put a loop on the seven." Alex pulled a paper out of his pocket and looked at it again. "It still looks like a nine. Here, look."

"Forget it!" Jules shook his head with disgust.

"I'm sorry I missed it, J. J." Alex continued. "Do you have a copy? I'd love to read it."

"No copies. All extemporaneous. When you were a football star, were you always late for huddles, too?" Jules shook his head with disappointment.

"Nah! They always tapped me on the shoulder or grabbed my arm."

"Follow us to our house," Jules nodded to Alex, "and I'll fill you in."

"Deal." Alex agreed. "Did they serve dinner here?"

"No, just snacks."

"Great! Hilda is the world's best cook. How about it? Am I invited?"

"You came late just to get a free dinner. You don't give a damn what J. J. said." Jules shook his head with despair.

"Sure, I do, but you'll cut it to a couple of minutes when you tell me."

"Is it OK, my dear?"

"Why of course," Hilda smiled. "It's not extra work or time and it is extra conversation and pleasure."

"You and your guys want something to eat, too, Charlie?" Jules asked.

"Yeah sure, but they'll stay outside and eat."

"OK, come one and all." Jules smiled, and they walked to their cars. Jules' car was closest. He opened the door for Hilda and said to his friends, "Last one there is—"

Before he could finish, Charlie and his bodyguards leaped into their car and started quickly toward the exit. Alex who arrived late ran across the long lawn. He jumped into his car raced his engine, squealed his tires on the well-kept grass, in his effort to win.

There was no way for him to pass on the two-lane country streets of Mill Valley. Jules' eyes staid on the racers. Charlie's car turned to the right. Alex turned to the left because there was no way pass on the narrow two-lane streets on the steep hillside road. The race was on. Jules finally looked at Hilda, saw she was securely in the car, and closed the door. As he got in Hilda asked with slight disgust,

"Why did you have to do that?" Hilda asked.

"Competition is fun."

"But there's no way we can win."

"We can't lose. We have the key to open the front door. We can take our time and we'll be the winner. We'll be the first ones in the house."

Jules and Hilda drove slowly around and down the winding and hilly road to the valley and on to their house which was a small, grey brimstone house with two bedrooms and bathrooms set between two large white wooden houses which was the predominate housing style.

The house had been a wedding gift to them from J. J. Jules had become a superior employee and J. J. wanted them to feel part of his family. He gave them the house and deducted ten percent of Jules' paycheck every month for payment. When fully paid, the house was theirs, and of course, the higher the paycheck to Jules the sooner the payoff for J. J. It was a delightful deal for both.

"What did you think of J. J.'s message?" Hilda asked as they approached their home.

"I agreed with what he said, but I guess I was the only one." Jules shook his head with a smile.

Hilda nodded in agreement. Jules parked and walked around the car to open the door for Hilda as Hilda had instructed him on their first date.

Charlie's bodyguards blocked the door from Alex. Jules assumed Charlie had won. Alex stared at the two as if the football had been handed to him and he had to dive into the solid opposing line to make the touchdown. They couldn't stop him.

"Coming through." Jules edged his way between them and opened a passage for Hilda to enter the house first. Alex followed tight behind them. His line had opened a hole. He scored the touchdown. He'd won.

DINNER TIME

As they sat at the dinner table, Alex asked, "What the hell did J. J. say?"

Jules gave a brief summary. As he ended, Charlie added, "The only ones who applauded were Jules and Hilda. Everyone else just wanted to get the hell out of there. No one was happy."

"I sure as hell was." Jules looked angrily at Charlie. "By the way, when the hell did you become a Muslim? You were over for dinner at Christmas. You weren't a Muslim then."

"I'm a slow learner. My eyes used to constantly look for police. Not anymore. It's as if I'm their best friend. I could carry an automatic rifle under here," he shook his large white robe, "and ten pounds of cocaine and walk through any police station and all would smile approval at me and ignore me. I'm invisible to the police. Hell, you know what? In public schools they're now teaching religion, but only the Muslim religion. Everyone's going to be invisible."

"That ought to scare you," Jules replied.

"Not me—you! I'm part of the gang. You are not. You are now the problem. If you're smart, you'll join us."

"Obama wanted everyone to be Muslim," Alex added. "So what? What the hell difference does it make what religion you are?"

"As J. J. pointed out," Jules said, "they want to convert everyone to become Muslim. If you don't convert, they'll kill you. It's their belief. There's no discussion. You either convert or die. All the wars and killing today are Muslim based."

"So why fight it?" Alex asked. "Join them, live, the wars will stop. It sounds like a simple solution. None of us ever went to church anyway. So now we don't go and we say we're Muslim. Big deal! No killings, no wars, no problems. It's fine with me."

"If you're Muslim," Hilda spoke up from the kitchen, "you're always in church. You must be on your knees with your brow on the ground multiple times a day praying. Your religion becomes your life. You're no longer free. Jules, help me with these plates."

"OK, so he loses the Muslim vote. There's not enough in California to swing an election." Alex observed as Jules placed the food on the table. "But why the hell did he bring it up? What good does it do anyone especially him?"

"He just wanted to point out," Jules replied, "that we are a Christian nation which grants us freedom. J. J. pointed out what our free society has produced in comparison to all the other religious societies in the world. We are unique."

"Well what a joke!" Alex laughed. "Science has proven there is no God. The whole thing's a stupid joke."

"I think we've covered J. J.'s talk completely." Hilda said with a calm, pleasant voice. "Let's change the subject and enjoy our company and dinner."

The following day the newspapers printed the entire speech of J. J. They were shocked at the outcome. Instead of fury and righteous indignation, J. J. became a champion and his popularity began to skyrocket.

Six days later, the newspapers headlines were, "SENATORIAL CANDIDATE FALLS TO HIS DEATH IN HIS HOME."

THE MEETING

JULES WAS ALWAYS HURRYING. First and most important he had to get black coffee, two donuts for Hilda, and the morning paper, put on his running shoes and outfit, and drive across town to his preferred fire trail where he could take his half hour run. When his workday was finished, and he could relax at home, Hilda would fill him in on all the interesting news from the paper and all else.

It was a cool Spring morning around six thirty and the sun was just starting to rise. It was light enough for Jules to be able to see the elevated rocks and roots to avoid tripping. The first rays of sun brightened the peak of Mt. Tam. Jules made the first half of his run and started back. He expected to say "hello" to J. J. and his dog, Moresee, on his return, but surprisingly they were not there. Odd. They were always here. Something must be wrong with Moresee, Jules concluded. J. J. would be here regardless of how he felt.

Jules hurried to his car, hurried home, hurried his shower, hurried his change of clothes, swallowed his breakfast, kissed Hilda good-bye, hurried to his car, hurried to pick up Alex, but as usual waited four minutes for always late Alex. Then, they started the half hour drive to Petaluma. Jules no longer complained about his waiting for Alex. That was now normal and accepted.

"What's new?" Jules asked.

"I looked at some new cars yesterday."

"What make?"

"Ford. I want American."

"What kind?"

"I don't know. Maybe a SUV."

"You don't need all that room and they're expensive."

"Yea, I know. They all are. Maybe you could convince J. J. to give me a good raise. I haven't had much for over a year."

"I didn't see J. J. this morning. Moresee must be sick. J. J. is always there rain, shine, in sickness and in health. I don't know how he does it, but he does."

"Will you talk to him?"

"Shit, Alex! How much is the car you're looking at?"

"I don't know exactly. It's pretty good, I guess over thirty."

"Come on! Wake up! Your dad gave you the car you have. You get a free ride to work from me. Why the hell do you need a new car? You have a free car with no payments. Hell, I pay more than twelve hundred a month on this car. You're a lucky guy. I envy you. Most of the country envies you. Why do you want to get into debt?"

"I've got a six-year-old car. I want a new one, and I want it to be mine. I don't want to owe my dad or mom one damn penny. When that's done, my next deal will be I'm moving out."

The conflicting views continued until they drove into the parking lot of J. J.'s company. It was a low building that covered acreage. It spread out like king sized bedsheet on a carpet. The parking lot was huge and had much more room than taken by the current thirty or forty parked cars and vans. Jules and Alex were twelve minutes early and took their time toward the employee entrance. The race to work was over. Jules had won and now he could take his time. Surprisingly, they were greeted at the entrance by one of their delivery men who told them to go to the gymnasium.

Jules looked at him for a moment and was going to question him but refrained, nodded and they headed toward the gym. What was so damn important for everyone to go to the gym?

The gym was a basketball court with nets at either end. Blocking the right basket was a volley ball court. The seating was four rows of concrete with three concrete steps to get to each row. They were in time to be able to sit on the third row. The concrete was hard and cool.

Dolph more than covered his wooden seat on the edge of the court. His excess flowed over all sides. Behind him stood his trio of

Angela, Roy, and John Peter Shielding III. Dolph kept glancing at his wristwatch and finally stood up and tapped the microphone to be sure it was working. He cleared his voice twice.

"Close the doors." Dolph instructed the men at the doors. "Get the names of all who are late. Tell them they are late and cannot enter." Dolph cleared his throat again. "I want to know who they are." After a slight moment he continued.

"This is a terribly tragic day." Dolph lowered his voice and put his chin on his chest. "I'm sure you've all read or heard about the tragedy. If you haven't, I must sadly inform you that Mr. Jerry Jackson had a terrible accident last night. He tripped and fell over the hall bannister to his death." He paused.

Jules stiffened. His eyes widened to their fullest. How could this be true? It couldn't be true. It was impossible. J. J. was too short to fall over that high bannister. What the hell was going on? This was crazy. It was a lie.

"To sum it up," Dolph shook his head and the fat danced around his mouth, chin and throat, "the police have determined Mr. Jackson's death to be one hundred percent the result of an unfortunate and tragic accident caused by Mr. Jackson himself. The police have determined that the case is officially closed."

Dolph Briskie's eyes searched every face up and down the concrete rows in a defiant manner. John Peter Shielding III, stood motionless and his eyes stared straight ahead. Angela tried as usual to smile but today it was slightly twisted as if trying to display deeper feelings. Roy Butler wore a challenging smile. He looked over the audience ready for a fight.

"Any rumors to the contrary," Dolph continued, "that you might read or hear are completely unfounded. There is NO question about his death. IT WAS A TRAGIC ACCIDENT. Mr. Jackson fell over the balcony of his mezzanine to the marble floor of his foyer last night, Thursday, and died instantly. His neck was broken on impact with the marble floor. He suffered no pain. It is a terrible shock to all of us and all his friends. He was greatly loved and will be missed by all. May he rest in peace.

"We all work in the company Jerry Jackson and I founded. He had the money to start it, and I had the sales knowledge to make it grow. I have been instructed by the new owners to take Mr. Jackson's role as President.

"We must remember one thing only. All of us are being paid to produce profits for this business. All things that distract from this are costly and bad to the business. Therefore, idle discussion about his death is costly and bad.

"The case is closed. We know the correct answer to the unfortunate death of Jerry Jackson. It was an accident. The police have closed the case.

"In honor of Mr. Jackson, our new owners have given all of us the rest of today off. On Monday when you return to work there will be zero discussion of Mr. Jackson's unfortunate accident. Anyone who persists on talking about his death rather than doing their job will be terminated. You have the rest of today and the whole weekend to do all the discussion you want about Mr. Jackson's unfortunate death. Are there any questions or comments?"

Jules stood quickly and in a loud firm voice for all to hear, "J. J. was murdered. It was not an accident. He was murdered."

"Mr. Cameron please see me in my office now. Anyone else?"

Alex stood and calmly said, "I agree."

"Anyone else want to leave this great company?"

The gym was silent. Most were afraid to breathe. Dolph continued.

"Our stock price may be temporally affected, but please ignore that. It will bounce back quickly. That is all! It was a terrible, shocking loss, but accidents

happen. I will act, until the board meets next year, as your new president. Give some silent prayers for Mr. Jackson when you have a few spare moments after work. In the meantime, please go home and remember how much Mr. Jackson loved each and every one of you." Dolph's fat fingers clumsily searched for the button to turn off the mike. The mike let out a scream before becoming silent.

Jules and Alex waited for the gym to empty to follow Dolph and his troupe to his office.

"This is great!" Alex said happily.

"How?" Jules asked.

"I didn't like this job anyway. Damn, it was more boring than Dolph. Now I'm going to be a famous detective. What's the pay?"

"A 'thanks' every time you do something right."

They followed silently behind Dolph and his gang. Jules was thinking about no money coming in with their baby on the way. This couldn't have happened at a worse time. Alex was thinking of exciting times ahead. This was going to be fun.

THE OFFICE

Roy opened the door to what had been J. J.'s office. Dolph entered first with the air of a king, then J. P. Shielding, Angela, and Roy closed the door behind. The reception room was small, and the receptionist was young and attractive.

"Wait here." Dolph instructed. "I'll call you shortly." They entered his office.

"I guess you've been here a bunch of times," Alex said to Jules when the office door was closed. "This is my first time." He walked up to the receptionist. "Hi, my name is Alexander Tyler, call me Alex. I was drafted by a pro team after college to play linebacker for them. The summer before showing up I broke my leg in a motorcycle accident. Dumbest thing I ever did. That was the end of my football career and now I'm starting a new life. Are you married?"

"No." was her curt reply.

"How about going out for dinner in a nice restaurant sometime?"

"I currently have a boyfriend."

"Good! He can come, too. I just find you fascinating and need to learn more about you. Come on—please!"

Her buzzer rang. She quickly picked up the device, turned it off, and nodded to Jules and Alex. "You may go in now." Her cold professional expression remained frozen on her face.

What's your name?" Alex asked as Jules headed toward the door.

"Linda." She almost whispered.

"And where do you live?"

"Terra Linda."

"They must have named the city after you. It's a beautiful town and area." With that, Alex followed Jules into what used to be J. J.'s office.

Everything in J. J.'s office had been designed for his slight stature. His desk was a dark, polished mahogany in a "U" shape. J. J. didn't have to move his chair to touch every part of the "U." Now Dolph was in the chair behind the "U." The arms of his chair became hidden with Dolph's huge arms. The desk's "U" became a tight fit for him. Roy stood by the door. Angela took a seat with notebook and pen outside the right of the "U." J. P. Shielding was seated slightly behind Dolph on his left.

"Mr. Cameron," Dolph started, "you and Mr. Tyler may stay if you each write an apology that we can hand to each employee. In it you must state how sorry you were to make such an erroneous statement. You can use whatever reason you want for being so foolish. It can't be just one letter written by both of you. You must each write your own apology. Is that clear?"

Jules smiled to himself. He was now "Mr. Cameron." Alex had gained importance, too.

"Maybe I was wrong, Mr. Briskie." Jules replied in a soft kind voice. "It probably was an accident as the police claim. But what if they were wrong? What if J. J. had been murdered and the new facts became true and absolute? If the police or someone else could point to someone and say 'this is the murderer and this is how the murder was done'. Don't you think that would stop all conjecture and conversation? Look at all the motives for murder. J. J. had insulted myriad groups. He had just come into a ton of money selling his company. Maybe someone would gain an important position by his death." He smiled at Dolph.

"What the hell are you insinuating? Damn it, Jules, how can you say such a thing and look hard at me?"

"I'm not implying anything, Mr. Briskie. I do have an idea that would be good for everyone. Why don't you give Alex and me our two-week vacation starting now? If we can't prove anything in two weeks, it'll all be forgotten. How about it?"

"Ha!" Dolph snorted. "Are you and Alex going to write your letters stating how wrong you were to doubt the police and apologize to all?"

"How can we write letters when we're unsure of the truth?"

"You, Mr. Cameron, have been treated like a spoiled child around here. J. J. let you get away with everything. He treated you as if you were the boss and everyone had to listen to you. Well, Jules you are not the boss. I am. We can do very well without you and your friend, Alex. No vacation time for either of you. You are both fired. Try to find someone else who will treat you like J. J. did."

"J. J. was the father I never had." Jules replied. "He gave me this job so Hilda would marry me. She and J. J. became the missing love I never had. I owe him a lot. No, I owe him everything. If it wasn't an accident, I have to find out who murdered him. You want to write the letter, Alex?"

"Hell no! We're a team. We've got a new job." Alex was smiling. This was going to be fun.

"Open the door for them, Roy, and good-bye and bad luck." Dolph was upset.

As the door closed behind them, Alex went straight to Linda. "I can't take you out for a nice dinner if I don't have your phone number."

Linda hesitated, looked again at Alex, then took a slip of paper previously written and handed it to Alex. He threw her a kiss as they walked out the door.

They walked in silence to Jules' car. As they got in, Alex asked, "How are you going to tell Hilda, Partner?"

BACK TO MILL VALLEY

As Jules slid behind the wheel of his car, Alex was already seated.

"Do you think Dolph murdered him?"

"When you don't know the answer, anything can be true."

"You think his fat ass could make it up those stairs? I don't."

"He could make it. Slowly, sure, but he can and could do it. When there's enough motive, anything can be done. He had super motives—money, power, and revenge. Dolph did the work and brought in the sales—J. J. got the rewards."

"Dolph had a good job. He didn't have to do much. He must have made a big salary."

"I'm sure he did, but he was always second class."

"What class are you? You ain't got no stinking job now."

"I'm in the same class as you. Why the hell did you quit? You didn't have to do that. Your dad is going to chew your ass."

"I'm right where I want to be. Do you think I was having a great time putting away inserts, taps, drills, and all that other shit for the past three or four years? I was going to be a football star and I end up doing that crap. Wow! I'm out of it. Now I'm going to be a famous detective with you. I can see the sign on the door—TYLER and CAMERON. I deserve top billing, right? Besides, Alex comes before Jules in the alphabet."

"Then the sign should say, ALEX and JULES in our jail cell."

"No problem. I can handle that."

"Look, Alex, this isn't a game or a joke. J. J. was murdered. I'm sure of that. We have a serious and dangerous job. If he or she murdered once, they will have no problem murdering again and since the police closed the case as an accident, then we're the ones in line to be murdered. If you're not aware, you could be next and I sure as hell don't want that."

"We're safe. Nobody knows."

"That's right. Except for the hundred or so people in the gym. They all heard me. They saw you back me up. If the murderer is one of them, we're in their sights. If not, word will spread about what happened and we'll be watched carefully. Damn it all, Alex, keep your eyes open. Pretend you're in a football game. You're carrying the ball for a touchdown. You only need seven yards. You have an opening. It looks like clear sailing. You're going to make it and win the game. Two yards short of the goal line you're hit in the side where you're holding the ball. The ball spirts out. You are downed one yard short. You lose the game. You lose everything. This is serious business, Alex, you knew football as well or better than anyone. Neither of us know this business. Everything is at risk including our families."

"OK, I'm scared. I'll suspect everyone. OH my God! Maybe you're the murderer. You killed him, didn't you? All this other stuff you did was just to remove your guilt. Don't shoot me, Jules. I'll shut up."

"If I had a gun, I might. What are you going to tell your dad?"

"Easy. I quit, and I've decided to become a detective. OK now that I am one, what the hell are we going to do next? You've got to remember I'm new at this. Where do we start?"

"I saved the newspaper where they copied his speech word for word. I'm going to read it carefully and try to figure out who he hurt the most. That's where we'll start."

"When do you figure that's going to be?"

"Bright and early tomorrow. Be ready. Bring your own car."

"It's a deal, but wait a minute. You asked me about what dad would say. That's nothing. What the hell is Hilda going to say? She's pregnant and could lose everything. You could be out on the street begging. Don't worry I'll throw you a dime and maybe mom and dad will, too. We'll take care of you, old pal. I just mention you because Hilda is smart. She can get any man she wants and she doesn't want to live on the streets with a loser. What are you going to tell her?"

"Old pal, you'll never know." Jules stopped to car in downtown Mill Valley. Alex looked at Jules and hesitated getting out.

"OK, you win for now. You know, it's still early. I'm sure everyone has left the plant except Dolph. I'm sure he did it. Why don't we go back and talk to him now without his three stooges."

"Come on! We just left there."

"But Dolph will be sitting behind his big desk in his big office all alone and his chest will be swelling bigger than his ass. That's a lot."

"I've got to talk to Hilda. Call me tomorrow around eight and I'll tell you our plans."

"How about the dinner tonight?"

"Seven. Tell Charlie, too."

"Sure. Lucky me. No job, no food, and I do all the dirty work."

Alex got out of the car carefully, nodded agreement, then looked worried, turned around twice as if to see who was following him, let out a loud sigh of relief, smiled, waved to Jules, and sauntered to his car.

HILDA

Hilda rushed to see who was at the front door. On her way she inspected each piece of furniture, the rug, lamps, to find if any speck of dirt or dust. Oh, my goodness! Something's hanging from the lampshade. She was sure she had wiped that yesterday. How had she missed it? She would attend to it after seeing who was at the door. No, she would do it now. It was a spider web. She looked for the spider but didn't see one. She was pleased with that. She hated spiders. Another knock and Hilda opened the door.

"Hi, Jenny. Come on in."

Jenny looked distraught. "Have you heard the terrible news?"

"I guess not since I haven't read the newspaper or listened to TV this morning. What is it?"

"Mr. Jackson died last night. He fell off his balcony."

Hilda reached for something to support her. She grabbed the door handle. "Oh, my God!"

Jenny rushed to her side and led her to the closest chair. Jenny sat down across from her. Jenny put her elbows on her knees, her head in her hands, and looked across at Hilda with almost a smile as she watched Hilda's shock.

"What happened?" Hilda shook her head as if the cobweb on the lamp had now encircled her brain. "How did he die?"

"He tripped and fell off his balcony onto the stone floor of the foyer. I guess he broke his neck and died instantly."

"Oh my, how terrible! That's just terrible! He was Jules' hero. Jules is going to be crushed."

"Of course he is. But how about you? What's going to happen with this house? Will you be able to stay?"

"We'll worry about that later. The most important thing now is Jules."

"You're wonderful, Hilda, but you have to think beyond the present. It would be terrible if you had to move in the condition you're in."

Hilda was silent and then smiled. "Are you offering us a place at your house? That's so sweet and thoughtful, Jenny."

"Well, no! That's not what I meant. Of course, if you need a temporary place to stay, that could be worked out."

"Do you have a bassinet I could temporarily use? He or she will be due in about four months."

"Oh, Hilda, why must you always make light of things?"

"Because the important thing right now is Jules. What did the paper say about Mr. Jackson?"

"A few nice things. A lot of not so nice things."

"Like what?"

"Well, he gave generously to certain groups who could help him financially, and nothing to other groups."

"How terrible for him to be a sensible man."

"Well, it wasn't that he just didn't give to certain groups, he verbally attacked them."

"Like who?"

"Blacks, Muslims, and the scientific field."

"So the press is saying he was a kind, generous, gentle evil bigot."

"He was a cruel bigot. Here's the paper. Read about him. He may have been nice to you, but he sure wasn't to a lot, and I mean a lot, of people."

Hilda could see she was trapped. If she supported Mr. Jackson, she would become a fellow bigot. "Thank you, Jenny. I'll look forward to learning the truth."

There was a moment of silence. Jenny stood and tried to force a smile. "I'm so sorry about Mr. Jackson's death. I hope Jules will be OK. Let me know if there's anything you need."

"Thank you, Jenny. You're a true friend. Thanks for coming over and thanks for the information. It's interesting to find out what the paper thinks is the truth. Remember when they were actually NEWS papers?"

Jenny smiled, nodded, and left.

After Jenny left Hilda read the article. In it, Simon Jones, a black leader claimed he had asked Mr. Jackson for a donation and had been told,

"The government gives you billions every year. What have you done with it? Have you made your communities a place where everyone wants to live and the real estate prices are going to the sky? I don't think so. How could a few dollars from me help when billions from the government hasn't?"

A Muslem leader, Hasham Kashi, said he had been refused a donation because, "All the wars in the world are caused by Muslims. I donate to God and peace not to wars and killing."

Joseph Mac Neal, a leading scientist in the Earth's origins was told, "If the creation of the world was an accident and accidents have zero consistency, then why is everything consistent? All the planets and stars are round. None are square or other shapes. All life reproduces its own and what it produces remains identifiable, unique, and the same generation after generation. Also, evolution is a farce, a joke. There has been more than a million years of life. If evolution started, it wouldn't end. Therefore, after a million years, evolution should be at its peak now. There should be things evolving all around us, but nothing—not one thing, is evolving into something else. Evolution is a lie and I won't donate to perpetuate your dangerous and reckless lies."

Hilda heard Jules drive into the easement, put down the paper, rushed to take that piece of dust she had noticed earlier, and stood in front of the door to greet Jules.

HEEL, TOE AND AWAY WE GO

What were the odds that Jules and Hilda would be friends? Probably around a thousand to one. How about them getting happily married? Forget it. Impossible. Millions to one. Let's say their backgrounds were slightly different.

Jules was a deserted orphan. No parent claimed him. He was raised in multiple households because his adopted parents had problems between each other. He accepted the fact that all was temporary and he was alone. To get strength he decided he had to win—not at sports which were in teams—but in school classes. He decided to put all his efforts into getting the best grades and he did. He gained respect of his classmates.

After being graduated, several colleges offered him scholarships. Jules turned them down. He was finished with school. He had accomplished all he wanted. Going to college was a trip to nowhere. He didn't want to be a doctor, lawyer or whatever and to gain a profession was the only reason for college. Otherwise, after you were graduated, you'd owe thousands of dollars in loans. If you'd get a good job, the government slugs would take your money. They'd get fifty, sixty percent or more. The sleeping slugs working for government became the winners. You would spend your life working hard and your hard work allowed the slugs to sleep, drink, and have fun. They were the government Mafia.

He and Charlie Givens solved the problem. They formed a gang to sell marijuana and other drugs. Since Charlie was black and to avoid any thoughts of racial bias or discrimination, Jules named the gang the black and White, "B" got top billing. BW became their trademark.

Since it was illegal, they could keep as much money as they wanted and pay the government as little as possible. The gang was just starting to get successful when Jules met Hilda.

Hilda's background was somewhat conventional. She had been raised in a small town east of Sacramento and close to the mountains. Her father, whom she loved, died in a fall when she was sixteen. When her mother remarried a year and a half later. Hilda was furious and didn't like her new father regardless of all the nice and pleasant things he did especially to please her. When Hilda moved to Sausalito in the San Francisco Bay Area, her new father sent her all the money she wanted without complaint or hesitation. She liked taking the money from him but hated all contact with him.

One day Jules was working the park below Bay Street which is a large area of grass, benches, bay front, and beautiful views of Marin County, Angel Island. Alcatraz, the Golden Gate Bridge, the East Bay cities and of course, behind were sights of San Francisco. The sky was clear this day. The temperature was mild. The wind and fog were not screaming and streaming under the Golden Gate Bridge. All the scenery was vivid.

Jules noticed two young, attractive gals, nicely dressed, looking like they had money, and a thirst for fun and fantasy.

"Excuse me, ladies, but I think one of you dropped this." He held up a small plastic packet.

"Did you drop it, Gloria."

"No. I've never seen it before, Hilda."

"What's in it?" Hilda asked.

"Well, I don't rightly know." Jules said with a smile.

"Open it. Let's see."

Jules with fingers fumbling on purpose opened it and spread it out.

Gloria wrinkled her nose. "That looks like marijuana."

"Is it?" Hilda asked with feigned enthusiasm. He wants to play games. OK. Let's play.

"Yes, it is." Jules stepped forward and presented it to Hilda. "My name is Jules Cameron and here is my phone number. This is free but there's lots more available to you two."

Hilda pushed his hand away. "Oh, I don't want it. I just want information about it. I hear lots of stories and I don't know what's true. You're the expert. You must know."

"Like what?" Jules put the packet away and looked at Hilda.

"What does it do?"

"It makes you happy. It raises you up above the clouds. You get real high."

"For a day, a week—how long?"

"A few hours. Then you can take some more and rise even higher." Was she kidding?

"That sounds wonderful. Then I always have to get more and more?. Do I keep getting it free forever?"

Jules laughed but studied her eyes. She looked sincere. How could a sweet gal be so ignorant? Had she been raised in a convent? "If you want to keep happy, it costs you a bit. Not much, but happiness always has a price."

"Is it like a vitamin? Does it improve my health?"

'Some doctors prescribe it to lessen pain."

"I don't have any pain. What good is it for me?"

"It will erase all the pains of the day and make you happy."

"So any time I have a problem I take some and the problem is evaporated. Is that it?"

"Pretty much so."

"Then more problems I get the more I'll need it. It sounds like I'd become addicted and the drug would own me."

"No way. You'd always be happy and floating high above all your problems." Jules kept watching her eyes. He became convinced she was serious.

"How often do you take it?"

"I don't take it. I sell it."

"Please take some now so I can see exactly what happens."

Jules blinked. He'd been taken. Damn! He didn't like it. "Look, I'm sorry you're not interested. I've got to go."

"Please take some. I'll watch your reactions and your face. That might convince me to try it."

"Look lady," Jules took a deep breath and relaxed his shoulders. "I've never even tried it and I'm not about to start. See you."

"Just one more minute. If you don't take it, it must be dangerous. That means it could cause harm. So you try to destroy your customers? That doesn't seem like a good way to build a business."

Jules stood and stared at her. A good looking gal had beaten him. How could he lose to a woman? Finally, he said as calm as possible, "I sell them for relaxation, comfort and happiness just like a nice cocktail. You have some nice wine or something every now and then, don't you?"

Hilda nodded her head and smiled. The game was going well. "Would you like to get high with me?"

Jules stared at her. What the hell was this? "Sure, yeah, OK. Where do you want to go?"

"Over there." Hilda pointed to the Golden Gate Bridge.

"We'd get run over." Jules watched Hilda as if she were raising an ax.

"No, no. We wouldn't lie in the road. That would be silly. We'll climb to the top of one of those towers where the cables come down to hold the bridge. The view would be fantastic. We could see the East Bay, Marin County, San Francisco, and the great expanse of the Pacific Ocean. That would be a real high! Then we could kiss, hold hands, flap our arms and fly down into the traffic. What an exciting flight! Let's do it." Hilda put her hand to her forehead as if in rapture.

"Sounds great. Let's go." He reached for Hilda's hand.

She hastily pulled it away and became angry. She saw the game was over. "Please! You offered me a high. I'm offering you a higher high. In fact, it's the best possible high."

"You want to kill me. Am I that terrible?"

"We'd both die as would some people in their cars on the road. That would be a lot less people then the number you're killing now."

"OK. Thank you for the lecture. Can I go now?"

"Of course. Here's your card."

"No, no. You keep it. You now know my name, phone number, occupation, and how easily a lovely lady can buffalo me. I'd like the same from you."

"We've had our first and last fling. I don't want to associate with a person who will take someone's money and then kill them."

"I don't kill people. I give them pleasure like a good cocktail."

"If you were to pour a cocktail into your lungs, yes, you'd die. The alcohol goes into your stomach and your body disperses it. Your smoke goes only into the lungs. If smoking cigarettes causes cancer, how can marijuana smoke be good?"

"I think we should discuss this more. You've made some good points." Jules hated losing to a gal especially a beautiful one. This kind of gal never had to work or study, They'd get by all their lives on their beauty. How could he lose to her?

"You're on a one way street that leads to trouble and jail. I don't want to watch you destroy yourself and I don't want to join you in jail."

"What if I were to stop?"

"You already said you don't use it."

"I don't, but if you'll go out with me one time, I'll get another job."

"Selling cocaine?"

"No, something legal. Something you approve." He had to win.

Hilda was now unsure. Was he playing her? Was this another game? Was he really serious? He was nice looking and entertaining. He could be fun on a date, but she didn't want to associate with gangster types.

"You get the job. Tell me what it is. I'll check it out. If it passes inspection, we can discuss it further."

"You don't really trust me."

"You murder your customers."

"Not really. They're committing suicide."

"Why don't you tell them you're handing them loaded guns?"

"OK. I see where you stand. I understand, but please give me your name and phone number and if I change, I'll let you know. It won't be a game and I won't lie to you."

Hilda hesitated for a moment and then reached into her purse and wrote down his request. She was certain he would never change. "If you really don't lie, I'll never hear from you again. Good-bye." She looked down at his card and added, "Jules."

As Hilda and Gloria walked away, Jules shook his head but couldn't smile. He'd been taken by a beautiful gal. He had lost. Maybe he'd forget her soon. No way! He had to win.

He looked away from her and there was the Golden Gate Bridge. His eyes flew to the top of the towers. He imagined standing there with Hilda. They'd look down at the traffic. If they jumped into the traffic, it'd be a fantastic flight down. Yes, they'd both die. What if they jumped into the bay? Sure, they'd make a big splash—maybe break every bone in their bodies. There had to be a way to do it and live. He would figure it out. He would do it, and she'd be wrong. He would win.

He became haunted by those towers every damn day. He couldn't figure a way to jump and live without sails or some device.

He changed his course. He couldn't lose to a woman. He closed his eyes to the towers and took a new tack. On his daily morning run on the fire trail in Mill

Valley, there was an elderly guy named Jerry Jackson with his Airedale named Moresee. They were there every morning. Out of curiosity Jules had stopped and talked several times. After several months of talking, Jerry Jackson offered Jules a job in his company. Jules had thanked him and laughed it off. This morning was going to be different.

Jerry Jackson, an older white haired guy, was sitting on a log and Moresee was panting and lying beside him.

"Good-morning, Mr. Jackson."

"Oh, my God! You're getting formal. No more J. J.? Now it's MR. JACKSON? What gives?"

"You offered me a job before. Is it still open?"

"Did they throw you out of your own gang?"

"No, I'm thinking of quitting."

J. J. laughed. "You taking me for a sucker? Come on!"

Jules paused. Yes, he had been. Now what? He looked at the trees and the view of Mt. Tamalpais before responding.

"Yeah, I guess so. But now I mean it. I'm going to quit what I'm doing. Have you got a job for me?"

"Sure. Here's the deal. My wife, Lydia, the encyclopedia, died about seven years ago. We never had any kids. I like you despite your history. I'll hire you only

if you promise to do exactly what I tell you to do and no excuses. What do you say?"

"I say it's a deal. When do I start?"

"Tomorrow. You will be my prodigal son. You need a lot of straightening out, but I think it can be done. I saw your record in high school. I know a lot more about you than you can imagine. You could be good. You could be just what our

company needs. You'll get a good salary and I'll take care of you. You will be my prodigal son, but you must obey me. Is it a deal?'

"It's a deal."

J. J. rose and they shook hands. The deal was sealed.

J. J. was a tough boss. He instructed Jules on tooling, dress, manners, and everything of which he thought important for success. Jules had no problem with the instruction. He wanted to win. He wanted to beat Hilda.

J. J. was impressed with his progress. He was converting the prodigal son. He enjoyed Jules. Jules finally had someone who cared.

After his first week at work, Jules called Charlie, his partner in crime, and told him the black and white gang was Charlie's. Charlie argued shortly but then saw his monetary rewards and agreed with a smile. Jules then left a message on Hilda's phone three weeks later. Before agreeing to a date, Hilda wanted to meet and speak to his boss.

Jules explained the situation to J. J. He smiled and arranged for Hilda to come to the plant on Saturday. He hired a Rolls Royce to transport her. She met them at J. J.'s office in Petaluma.

Jules showed her around the warehouse of cutting tools and other items for machine shops. He showed her high speed, cobalt, carbide, and diamond cutting tools. He told her that they had to cut to tolerances and sometimes that meant as close as .0005 inches and sometimes to even closer. She was impressed with the company. Had Jules changed his life for her or was it another of his tricks?

She agreed to a first date. It was a success. Jules was going to teach her not to ever fool with him again. Then came the second date, third, and more.

Jules kept patting himself on his back. He was sure he was the winner. Yet it was Jules who got on his knees to Hilda, begging for her love, handed her an expensive engagement ring, and proposed they marry. Hilda smiled and nodded her approval. After their marriage, Jules still thought he had won.

Seven years had passed and now their first child was due in four months. Jules had a beautiful wife who fulfilled him greater than any mother he might have had. He had a good job and the closest thing he'd ever had as a father—J. J., and now he was about to be a father himself.

What an incredible reversal in his life. Now he had tell Hilda he'd lost his job. Their future, their house, their income, their enjoyable and comfortable life was about to end. He dreaded telling her anything that might hurt her in any way. This wasn't a minor situation. It was major. It was and would be devastating to her but she had to be told. That was necessary.

Jules straightened and steeled himself as he walked through the front door.

DECISIONS

HILDA RECOGNIZED THE SOUND of the car and rushed to the front door to greet her husband. He must be devastated by the death of J. J. As soon as the door opened, Hilda put her arms around him and kissed his cheek.

"I heard about J. J.'s death." She whispered.

"I guess it was big news in the papers."

"I'm sure it is, but it was Jenny who told me. Here's the paper. Why don't you sit down and read it and I'll bring you some tea?"

Jules sat in his overstuffed red leather chair and read the entire article three times before glancing at his iced tea. Hilda sat on the edge of her chair watching and waiting.

"J. J.'s death is one problem. We have more."

Hilda said nothing.

"I don't know what to do. I am certain that J. J. was murdered. I told Dolph that and I got fired. Alex, for some damn reason agreed with me and he got fired, too. I'm out of a job. I guess I'll get two week's pay, but then, who knows. We may lose this house. I don't know. Of course, we may lose it anyway with the death of J. J. Regardless, I can't let someone get away with murdering him."

"Of course not! You did the right thing. Who do you suspect?"

"That's the worst part. Just reading the newspaper report, they keep bringing up the talk he gave to start his senate race. Even though he's surging in the polls now, they're trying to show that the whole world hated him and it's fortunate he died accidentally, or he would have surely been murdered."

"And what do you think, dear?"

"That's another worst part. I don't know. I don't even know where or how to begin. Damn, I don't think there are any good parts."

"Why don't we start at the beginning, dear."

"Great! But where the hell is that?"

"J. J.'s house. We can talk to his butler, Oliver, and his brother, Paul."

"When do you want to do that?"

"Let's do it now." Hilda smiled and took his arm as if he were in charge.

Jules ignored his iced tea, rose, and headed for the car. Hilda kept loving hold of his arm.

They drove in silence to J. J.'s house. Jules kept going over all Dolph had said earlier. Yes, Dolph had a good motive to murder J. J., but damn, he should have kept his thoughts to himself. That had been dumb, but then he thought of all the benefits Dolph now had and he thought Dolph was a good solid suspect.

As they pulled in front of J. J.'s house, Hilda waited for Jules to open the door for her. It was one of the rules to transform him. He didn't object. It was what she wanted—no problem.

There was one police car still in front of the mansion. Probably final clean-up work, Jules assessed. Oliver opened the door on the first ring.

"Ah, master Jules and the lovely madam Hilda. How good to see you. Please come in."

"It's nice to see you, too, Oliver. What a terrible tragedy. Are you all right?" Jules asked with deep sympathy.

"I'm as fine as possible under the circumstances, thank you, sir."

"May we come in and talk a bit?"

"Of course, sir. To whom do you wish to speak?"

"To you, Oliver."

"Very well, sir. I'm in the process of getting my things in order for my eventual return to England, sir. I don't think Mr. Paul will want my services."

"We'll want to talk to him, too and we'll let you know the information he gives us."

"That's very kind of you, sir, May I suggest we go to my quarters since the police are in and out of here on an irregular basis."

"That would be just fine, Oliver." Hilda gave him a soft smile. "How many years did you for Mr. Jackson?"

"Twenty-two years, madam. They were very good years. Mr. Jackson was always fair and honest. We had no problems. I shall miss him greatly." He ushered them to the great winding staircase.

"I'm sure he'll take good care of you in his will." Hilda used her soft compassionate voice.

"That would be nice, madam Hilda."

Jules stopped in his walk up the circular staircase. Of course! Oliver must be in the will. J. J. had just received three hundred and fifty million bucks. If Oliver got ten percent, that was thirty-five million bucks. If he only got one percent that was three and a half million bucks. Jules stopped climbing the staircase and looked down at the marble floor. Oliver would have no problem lifting J. J. over the bannister. His rewards would be in the millions. He would be the only person in the house, leave no incriminating evidence, so he was in the clear and rich.

"Are you all right, dear?" Hilda asked.

"Yeah, sure. You woke me up."

Hilda gave him a questioning look. No response. She walked on.

To the right, when on the balcony, was J. J.'s bedroom. They turned to the left to Oliver's quarters. He unlocked the door and stood aside for them to enter.

How unusual, Jules thought, for him to lock his bedroom door.

The bedroom was more like a library. There were bookshelves on all walls and each shelf was full. Oliver's bed was in the middle of the room. Behind the bed was a large floor lamp. On the right side of the bed was a table and at the end of the bed were two wooden chairs. Other than that, the room was bare. Not even a carpet on the wooden floor.

"Pardon my room please, madam and sir. As you can see, I'm not used to important guests."

"It's a unique and sensible bedroom." Hilda approved. "Thank you, Oliver."

Jules went to the end of the bed, spun the two chairs around, offered one to Hilda, and took the other for himself. Oliver stood by the side of his bed.

"How can I help you, sir?"

"I'm looking for the truth of J. J.'s death. The common assessment of his death is either accidental or suicidal. I think he was murdered, and I want to find out who did it. What can you tell us of that night, Oliver, that might help us?"

"I wish I could, sir. I honestly wish I could, but it was my night off. I went to the movies here in Mill Valley. It was a comedy about a guy and his unruly dog. When I returned, Mr. Jackson was lying on the marble foyer—dead. I called the police. That's all I know, sir."

"Did you come straight home after the movie, Oliver?"

"Not exactly, sir. I stopped at the corner bar and enjoyed a few."

"Does Paul have Moresee now?" Hilda asked.

"No, no, madam Hilda. Mr. Paul does not like dogs. Moresee was taken to the pound immediately.

"Doesn't anyone want him?" Hilda was concerned. "He'll be dead in a few days if just left there. Jules, we can't allow that."

Jules nodded. Damn! He had never had a dog and sure as hell he didn't want one now.

"Probably so, madam Hilda. He was a wonderful dog and I would gladly take im if I weren't returning home to England shortly."

"When do you plan to leave, Oliver?" Jules asked.

"When all the paperwork is finished."

"Could you please stay for at least three weeks?" Jules asked. "I'm sure I'll need your excellent help in solving J. J.'s murder."

"I'll do my best, sir, but I don't want to ruin my paperwork. It is so difficult to obtain."

"Thank you for your time, Oliver. We'll go down and see Paul now and if he does want to keep you on, I'll let you know."

"That would be most kind of you, sir."

PAUL JACKSON

OLIVER LET THEM OUT and they walked along the pebble path over the hill and down toward the guest house where Paul lived.

Hilda asked, "What did you think?"

"I think three hundred and fifty million bucks are in play. With J. J. dead, Oliver is a rich man regardless of the percentage of his cut. If he just gets one percent, that three and a half million bucks. He's set for life."

"That's true," Hilda agreed, "but Paul should be even richer being J. J.'s brother. Since J. J. had no children and no wife, Paul must be getting the biggest part of the inheritance."

Jules nodded to himself. That was so. They walked past the main house, and down a slight curve to the large guest house. Jules knocked loudly three times. No response. He repeated it four more times. Still no response. Finally, he turned the door knob. It was open. Hilda moved back in worry. Jules put his arm around her and they entered an anteroom.

"Paul Jackson!" Jules shouted. "You have visitors."

No response.

"I hope you're here. I hope you're OK."

A door opened and Paul entered. He was thin, muscular and almost as tall as Jules. His long, sharp face was scowling.

"How the hell did you get in?"

"We knocked several times," Jules replied calmly, "and there was no response. Since your brother, J. J., was murdered, we feared for you. The door was unlocked and we entered. We're delighted you're safe."

"Bullshit! He wasn't murdered. It was an accident. You know more than the police? You smarter than the experts? What the hell do you want?"

"First, we wanted to be sure you were OK because I'm sure J. J. was murdered.'" Jules kept his voice as calm as possible.

"I'm not going to fall over any damn bannister and die. Get the hell out of here. You're nuts."

"J. J. didn't fall over that bannister. That bannister came almost up to his chest. He'd have to climb up on it and jump."

"OK, he committed suicide. What the hell is the difference anyhow? He's dead."

"We feared the same accident or suicide might have happened to you. We wanted to be sure you were safe. When you didn't answer our knocks, we got worried. We're glad you safe. We want to make sure you stay that way."

"What the hell, do you want me to thank you for breaking in? No way! That's it. Case closed. Now get the hell out of here before I call the police."

"We're here to help you." Hilda said softly.

"You could help me a lot, Baby. What'cha got in mind?"

"Keeping you safe."

"Great! Come over here Baby and keep me safe. I'm scared, really scared. Please help me." He extended his arms as enticement. Hilda looked away.

"Do you know anyone who wanted to harm J. J.?" Jules asked.

"Damn right! The whole world. He made enemies fast. He was the best."

"Maybe it's now your time. You should be real worried."

Paul eyed Jules and saw there was no way he could take him. "Forget it! What the hell do you really want?" He wanted to somehow hurt him.

"Please gentlemen, please calm down." Hilda said in her softest voice. "We just need some simple answers and then we'll get out of your way."

"Name them." Paul put on his best smile.

"Could we sit down for a moment?" Hilda's voice became terse and hard.

"Yeah. OK. But just for a few minutes."

"Agreed." Jules replied.

Paul led them into his living room which was a play room equipped with pool table that was covered with a ping pong table top. Hilda sat in wooden chair by the pool table. Before sitting, Paul's eyes drifted to the pool cue rack. Jules watched and remained standing.

"I am Jules Cameron and this is my wife, Hilda. I was employed by J. J. He was like a father to me. I believe he was murdered. J. J. took care of us. I feel it's my duty to take care of him. I hope his death was an accident. If not, I want to find his murderer."

"He was more than kind to us." Hilda added. "No one has ever done the remarkably generous deeds that he has done for us. He bought our house and we pay him ten percent of our salary for repayment. As our salary goes up, so goes his payment. He was a wonderful man. You now own our house and we hope you will continue the precedent."

"So who do you think killed him?" Paul winked at Hilda.

"We have no idea." Hilda replied. "We're hoping for help from you, though."

"Where were you that night?" Jules asked.

"So I'm a fucking suspect, right? You, ass hole, should shut up and let your lovely wife do the talking. You have a lot to learn. Oh, let's see—Jules, Jules oh that's right Jules Cameron. You're the drug king, right?"

"Was." Jules kept his stern eyes on Paul. "That was years ago. J. J. converted me. There are many reasons I owe J. J."

"What a deal! He gets you out of drugs and puts you in his business. You're a lucky guy, Drug King."

"You're right." Jules nodded. "You and I are about in the same spot. Look what he's given you. Do you do any work at all? Hell no. You sit down here, play pool or whatever all day. He pays for it— pool, women, or every whim. I had a good deal but it can't compare to yours. And now you get rewarded for your hard working brother's death. He's dead. You're rich. What are you going to do with all that dough?"

"Hell, I don't know. Poor me—I inherited a ton of problems. I'll probably have to hire some guy to manage the dough. He'll probably cheat me. Maybe I'll have to kill him." He let out a chuckle. "J. J.'s death is the death of me. He did the work. I had the fun. It was perfect. Now I'm stuck with stupid problems, taxes, and who knows what. I don't want to do any damn work. I want to be like the government bums. Get everything and do nothing. I hate work. I wish he were still alive. I wish I could bring him back to life. Poor me."

"Where were you when J. J. died?" Jules asked.

"Son of a bitch! I am a suspect! OK, Drug King. I bought a gal for a couple hours of fun. I don't remember her name. She was good looking but ugly compared to you." He winked again at Hilda. She was not amused. "We met at a bar in San Francisco in the Mission District and went to her apartment. She was great!"

"When did you get back here?" Jules asked.

"Hell, I don't know. The police were here. They can tell you when I got back."

"Do you think you'll move to the main house and hire Oliver?" Hilda asked.

"Hell no and hell no! What the hell do I want with a monster house like that? Where would I put the pool table and my things? I'd get lost up there. Everything I have would get lost. I'd have to hire people to find things for me."

"And how about Oliver? Would you hire him?" Hilda persisted.

"You got to be kidding. I'm going to stay right where I am. I don't need a damn butler here. I know where everything is. Why should I pay for nonsense? I pay for things that are fun for me—like beautiful women. You know, Hilda, I've never thought of marriage before, but now I'm considering it."

"I'm very happily married and I'm pregnant with my first child." Hilda was trying to contain her anger.

"Yeah, sure, but that's OK with me. I'd have a prize wife and child all at the same time. Super! Look, my dear, you'll be marrying a millionaire. You'll have no problems and I'll get you anything you want. You'll have a carefree, rich, wonderful life. Dump the Drug King. Think it over. You'd lose a druggie and win millions. You'd have a fabulous life. You'd be among the happiest women in the world. I'd make sure you were."

"Yes," Jules said sharply, "you're going to inherit a lot of money. You're going to be very rich. When you buy women, they then immediately become prostitutes. Hilda could never be that."

"Why don't you let her answer?"

"There's no need. I am her husband. I protect her from evil. You are evil."

"That's the Drug King's opinion. Let her speak for herself. What do you say, darling Hilda? Who do you want to live with—a druggie or a millionaire?"

"I couldn't have said it better than what my husband just said."

"For the moment I'll accept that. But things can get tough and change. Keep me in mind, my dear. But you. Drug King, how the hell could you ever suspect me? That shows what a fool you are on top of everything else."

"I've never known two brothers who didn't fight each other." Jules stared coldly at Paul. "Maybe you and J. J. were the first exception in history. I doubt it. Yes, you led a reckless and rotten life. Yes, J. J. paid for it. Do you think your rotten life style made J. J. happy? It didn't. Maybe living with you made him want to repair me. I don't know, but words could have been said between you two and one thing could have led to another and you, in fit of fury, could have easily picked him up, tossed him over the balcony, and then left to do some whoring to get an alibi. That's why you're a suspect. You are rotten."

"Wow! I'm no longer a suspect. I am guilty. So we go to court. What do you think the judge will decide? Let's see—the police judged the death an accident. You were not at the scene. You are not a detective. There were no witnesses. You have no proof otherwise. The only proof you could have is if I confessed to the crime in front of witnesses. Why should I do that when it didn't happen? You know what the judge would decide? You Drug King will be the one going to prison and you'll be sued for every cent you have. Your wife will be alone and impoverished. Don't worry, dear, I'll take care of you. By the way, the reason I was late greeting you at the door was I was looking for my cell phone. It took me a while to find it, but I did. I've recorded every word. You are finished. You are guilty. Now do me a favor. Get the hell out of here."

"How about Moresee?" Hilda asked as if she had not heard a word.

"Who?"

"J. J.'s dog."

"You asking about a damn dog at a time like this? Forget it!. Dogs are work. I hate them. I don't give a damn about him. He's gone. What else?"

"Please," Hilda used her quiet voice, "would you please keep the same arrangement on our house payments that we had with J. J.?"

"As soon as I inherit your house, I'll sell it. You can put in your bid, but I'll take anyone else's regardless of how much lower their price is. You're out. One exception, Baby, you'll always be welcome here." Paul laughed for the first time. It sounded vicious, but there was also a joy in it as if he relished his victory.

Without another word Jules and Hilda left.

MORESEE

THEY WALKED SILENTLY UP the slight hill on the gravel path, passed
J. J.'s house, and walked on level ground toward their car.

"Do you want me to stop before I get us into more trouble?"

"Heaven no!" Hilda let out a short joyous laugh. "You were right.
Everything you said was right. We're doing fine."

"But I'm not a detective. I have no legal right to question him like
a detective. He could sue us."

"The first thing you said was that we were concerned about his
safety. We came to make sure he was safe and sound. He converted
the conversation. When he admitted what he'd done the night of J. J.'s
death, he saved us."

"And what if he changes his recording to incriminate me?"

"I recorded it all from your first knock. If he alters his recording,
he'll be in deeper trouble."

"Do you think he might have done it?"

"Of course. Very easily. He's vicious."

"But even if he did, there's no way to prove it."

"I'm not worried. You'll find a way."

"Thanks for your confidence. Now what?"

"We have to get Moresee."

"Come on! We can't afford a dog. I have no job. We have a baby on
the way. We may have a crippling law suit. As Paul said, they take a lot
attention and care." He opened the car door for Hilda.

"Then we'll let Moresee be exterminated. I'm sure J. J. won't mind.
He's dead. I guess you feel Moresee wasn't that important to J. J. anyway."

Jules sat still for a moment behind the wheel. He looked at Hilda, glanced at his watch and saw twelve-fifteen, shook his head, smiled, started the car, and headed for the pound in San Rafael. On the way, he had to ask, "You got a pretty good offer from Paul."

"I hope you're kidding." Hilda's tone was sharp.

Jules stayed silent.

"When I was twelve, before becoming a teenager," Hilda continued, "my mother would tell me almost every night, 'there are two valuable assets in people, honesty and loyalty. They are rare. If you find one who has them, you have found a rare gem. Mercenaries and prostitutes are plentiful and common and have no value.' Paul has no value. You are my gem."

It was a one-story building that stretched out about a couple of hundred yards. They were greeted by a smiling, kind faced woman.

"How can I help you?"

"We're looking for an Airedale named Moresee." Jules replied.

"Oh, yes, we got him in yesterday. He's a problem dog. We're supposed to put him down as quickly as possible."

"Then you haven't done it." Hilda's eyes challenged the woman.

"No, it's scheduled for this afternoon."

"Good." Jules said. "We'll take him now."

"I don't know if we can do that." The woman replied. "He is listed as a dangerous and vicious dog. I don't know if he's allowed to be taken."

"May we see him?" Hilda asked.

"Of course. This way."

She led them past pen after pen of animals all of whom yearned for attention. Toward the end, she stopped and pointed toward Moresee.

"Hey, Moresee, how're you doing?" Jules put his hand through the bars and into the cage.

"No, no!" The woman shouted. "Be careful! Don't do that!"

Jules kept his hand in the cage. With wagging tail Moresee rushed to his hand. His nose ignored the possibility of food. He eagerly licked Jules hand.

"We'll take him." Jules said leaving his hand in the cage.

"I don't think so." The woman was confused and unsure.

"The whole reason for this building is for people to rescue animals," Jules observed. "We are rescuing Moresee. He loves me, and I love him."

"How about your wife and other people?"

Hilda moved quickly to the cage and inserted her hand. Moresee licked her hand. "We are safe with him and he is safe with us. We shall keep him under complete control so he won't injure or harm other people. Any injury to anyone would ruin us with law suits. You may be sure he'll be under complete control."

Jules petted Moresee the best he could through the bars. "We're old friends. We need to take him to our home."

"I'll have to check with higher authorities." The woman shook her head.

"We promise to fence our yard so he'll be safe and so will everyone else."

"And how will you handle him before the fence is in place?"

"I'm a stay at home wife. I'll keep him inside with me and will take him out on a leash only. I'll be sure everyone will be safe. I'm pregnant and my baby will need a dog for company and protection. We must have Moresee."

There was just a little more discussion and then Jules, Hilda, and Moresee were led back to the front office. The woman excused herself and went into another office. When she returned with a grim face she said, "You have been warned. It is in our records. You know the dangers involved. You may have the dog, but you must fill out these forms."

When all the official forms were filled, they were given a hangman's leash and they led a wagging tail Moresee to the car. He jumped in eagerly.

J. J. had told Jules why he had chosen an Airedale. President Teddy Roosevelt had loved Airedales because they are fearless, intelligent, and friendly. He decided to take his Airedales to Africa on one of his lion hunting trips. The problem was the fearless Airedales attacked the lion. Luckily, they were able to kill the lion before the lion killed his dogs. J. J. told Jules of another person he'd met on the fire trail with a giant Airedale. This person had been living in New York City and took his Airedale for a walk a little after five one morning. He kept his dog on a leather leash. As they rounded a corner, a man with a gun jumped out of a doorway and held him up. The Airedale broke the leather leash, knocked the guy flat on his back, and they calmly walked away. He never looked back to see if the guy had risen.

The last story Jules remembered was of a guy in LA who raised Airedales. He, his wife and his Airedale were sitting on their front porch. Across the street a Doberman was chasing a small dog. The Airedale dashed across the street, knocked the Doberman over, the terrier escaped, and the Airedale returned home. As Jules remembered this, his pride grew for Moresee.

As they arrived at their small house near the top of a hill in Mill Valley from which they could see parts of the bay and San Francisco, Hilda said quickly, "He might try to run back to his old home. We have to make him know that this is now his home."

Jules kept the hangman's leash around Moresee's neck and led the happy dog inside.

"OK," Jules said, "We have a dog. Now what?"

"Get acquainted. Take him to the fenced back yard. Play with him. Get him to realize that this is his home and you are his master."

Jules followed instructions and led Moresee outside. He sat down on a chair. Moresee looked at him. Maybe he should go to a sport store and buy some tennis balls. How else could he play with him? He thought for a while and then said, "OK, Moresee. This is what we're going to do. You probably won't like it and I know I definitely won't like it, but we're going to get to know each other." Jules went into the house and got a bar of soap and two towels. He turned the hose on lightly, took Moresee by the collar, and talked softly to him.

"OK, Moresee, this is how we're going to get acquainted and become close friends. You've got a new home. I hope you like it here and don't try to go back to your old house. Your dear master, J. J., is gone.

We're all you've got now. You can come with me on my morning runs, but you have to stay with me."

He started lightly hosing Moresee and petted him fondly all the while. As the water covered him, Moresee wanted to shake, but Jules held him tightly and then started rubbing him with soap.

"We have some things in common, old boy. You've lost your family. I never had one. I had several people try to save me, but it never worked. I hope this works with you. Your J. J. was murdered. I don't know about my real mom or dad. I never found out who they were or why they dumped me. It is almost impossible to find anyone who cares about you. Well, Moresee, you're lucky. You've found two people who care about you. You've got a new home. We're not rich like your J. J. In fact, we may be broke soon. One way or another, we'll keep you. You can rest assured that I'll protect you from any harm. You are part of our family just like our new baby is going to be. This is your home. You take care of us and I'll take care of you. Is it a deal?"

Jules was drying Moresee and Moresee was enjoying the rub down.

Hilda called out of the kitchen window. "Alex is on the phone. I told him what we'd done. He sounds a bit upset."

Jules squinted. Alex should have been included. He'd screwed up.

"Hey, Alex, sorry we went without you. Things happened fast and it slipped my mind."

"No problem." Alex said curtly. "You can tell me all about it on our way to see Dolph."

"The office is closed."

"I'm sure everyone's gone but Dolph. He's loving his new office and position. He'll be there. Tell you what. I'll drive. You can take Moresee. Hilda told me all about it."

"It's a deal, but I think you're wasting time and gas."

"Maybe. But I don't give a damn. Detectives like to take chances."

"OK detective partner, let's go."

"I'll pick you up in ten minutes."

Jules finished drying Moresee, patted his head, rubbed his back with both hands, and led him into the house.

"Moresee, you look beautiful." Hilda patted his head and went to the refrigerator, took out some hamburger, and offered it to him.

With a soft mouth he took the food from her hand. She offered more, and he delightedly took it. It didn't take long for Moresee to know and love Hilda. Jules told her what he and Alex were about to do. She smiled and said, "On the way back, you'd better go to the store and buy some dog food."

"Like what?"

"Just buy some kibble and I'll mix it with hamburger, oh and we're almost out of hamburger." The doorbell rang.

TWO DETECTIVES

Alex's jeans looked old and far from fresh. His white shirt was emblazoned with two letters that covered the width of the shirt—"ME."

"If Dolph is there," Jules said, "what makes you think he'll see us?"

"Hey! We've been fired. We'll walk right into his office. What can he do about it?"

"And what if big Roy is there?"

"I'll take him. You can take the rest. Angela might be fun."

"Have you ever been in jail?"

"Not yet. I guess you have."

"Wrong but we might be there together."

"OK. Let's find out. You and Moresee get the hell in and tell me what happened at with Oliver and Paul."

"I'm getting in the back seat with Moresee."

"You two deserve each other." Alex shook his head.

Jules talked directly to Moresee but his words were for Alex. When Jules finished a sentence, he'd pause, pat Moresee on the back or rub his nose and look deeply into his eyes. Moresee cocked his head in alternating positions trying to understand. He finally gave up and closed his eyes. Jules kept talking to him in a kind, gentle voice. He was careful to give Alex complete and accurate information of their visits with Oliver and Paul. He tried not to slant the information like the assassins do.

By the time he was finished, they were in Petaluma.

"What do you think about Oliver and Paul?" Jules asked as they got out of the car. Moresee started to follow. "You stay here and take care of the car." He rolled down all the windows and watched Moresee. Moresee just looked out and watched them leave.

"What's there to think? They're nothing. I tell you it's Dolph."

"Come on now! You're not using your head. J. J. sold the business for three hundred and fifty million bucks. If Oliver gets just a few percent, he's rich. Paul is going to get a lot. He'll be really rich. Oliver isn't a young kid and he wants to return home to England. Paul is a bum. He plays around and drinks. He and J. J. could have gotten into an argument. Paul could have been drunk, angry and thrown J. J. over the balcony. How can you dismiss that?"

"Easy. Dolph and company did it. It doesn't sound to me like Paul and Oliver are smart enough or have the balls to do it."

"Being smart has nothing to do with it. Self-interest is a key."

"There's plenty of that for Dolph and company."

"You're stuck on Dolph. How can you be a detective when your mind's already made up?"

"It must be Dolph and his gang. None of them liked J. J. being the occasional boss. Now if Dolph suddenly dies, we go right down the line. Look at how heavy Dolph is. It wouldn't be hard to arrange a heart attack or something. That would be easy. Roy could murder him. Angela could murder Roy, and John Peter Shielding could murder Angela. We'll be working on this for years."

They entered the main entrance and walked boldly to the president's office.

The receptionist looked at them. "Oh, hi again. May I help you?"

"Sure," Alex replied and stared at her for a long time before asking, "How about tomorrow night for our first date?"

"I beg your pardon!"

"I couldn't stop thinking of you. I had to see you again. I talked my friend into keeping me company. How about it?"

"I don't really know you. I think it would be best for you to leave."

"We met earlier, and I hoped you'd remember me. I'm Alex Tyler. I used to play football here, and then went on to play at the University…"

"Yes, Mr. Tyler. I remember."

"Great. We want to talk to Mr. Briskie for a minute. After we talk I'll ask you again for dinner tomorrow."

She got on her phone and in seconds Dolph Briskie waddled into the room.

"What's going on here?" He looked first at Alex and then at Jules. "You here to get your jobs back?"

"Can we talk about it?" Alex asked.

"Come on in but just for a few moments."

As they entered Briskie's office, Alex turned winked and threw a kiss towards Linda. She pretended she missed it, but she hadn't and behind her stoic face was a smile. Alex was large, powerful and nice looking. He could be fun, she thought, but he must have a thousand women. He was dangerous and intriguing.

As the door closed, Alex broke the silence, "We think you murdered J. J."

"Get out! Right now!"

"You've got a problem." Alex shook his head. "You and your receptionist are the only ones here. Jules wants to ask you some questions."

Dolph stared at Alex and then Jules. He stayed seated. He now had an extra wide chair. "I could call the police and you'd both be in deep trouble."

"Please don't." Jules said quickly. "We won't stop you from using your phone, but we're trying to clear up things. We have no idea who murdered J. J. Since we don't know, we must consider everyone a suspect. We're working on eliminating suspects and since we hold you in high regard, we want to eliminate you first. Can you tell us where you were the night of J. J.'s murder?"

"That's the first problem. You're wrong right off the bat. I'm glad I fired both of you. J. J. wasn't murdered. It was an accident or suicide."

"We believe it was made to look like that, but we don't believe it. Since we don't believe it, we have to look for people with reason to murder him. Wanting to take over his position would be a good reason."

Dolph sat still. Then he started shaking his fat face slowly. His cheeks bounced softly off his nose. "Angela, Roy, and I were at dinner at the 'X' Spot here in Petaluma. You want to see the receipt?"

"That would be great." Jules replied.

Dolph tried to get into his pockets but couldn't. With the help of the chair and his desk, he managed to stand. He finally found the receipt and laid it on the desk. Alex picked it up and handed it to Jules.

"This was an early dinner." Jules said. "The time was seven seventeen. Where did you go afterwards?"

"There was no place else to go. We discussed the terrible loss of J. J. and after eating we all went home."

"You are now a leading suspect." Jules said quietly. "How could you discuss his loss before he died? And it's odd you'd keep a two-week receipt."

"Come on! For God's sake! Get realistic. I put this receipt in my pocket in case the police asked for it. They didn't, but damn it you did. J. J. is always on my mind. Of course we didn't discuss his death at dinner. How the hell do you expect me to remember what was said at a dinner two weeks ago or even yesterday. My mind goes ahead. I can't remember the past or even what I had for lunch today. So I made a silly mistake. Of course we didn't discuss J. J.'s death. I don't remember what the hell we talked about. Now I'm a murderer? OK. I made a mistake. Arrest me. Then I'll sue the hell out of both of you."

"Relax, Dolph." Jules voice was soft. "You made a mistake. I appreciate that. We all make mistakes. I understand. Have you been out to dinner since J. J.'s death?"

"Many times." Dolph said coldly.

"Do you have all those receipts, too?"

Dolph was getting furious and was speechless. "That's for me to know and you to wonder. What else?"

"Were you, J. P. Shielding, Angela, and Roy all together?" Alex asked.

"If I remember correctly, yes, but my memory isn't the best."

"Do you have any idea where they went after dinner?" Alex asked.

"Ask them. Damn it all! It was an accident! Why are you trying to make something out of nothing?"

"J. J. took care of me." Jules replied. "It's my turn to take care of him. If I find out it was an accident or suicide, I'll be able to drop it and sleep. I have to find out the truth. Otherwise I'll never sleep.

Right now I'm suspicious of everyone. I need to eliminate the innocent and find the guilty. I would think you'd want to do the same. J. J. did a lot for you, too."

"This is going to have a bigger cost on both of you than you ever imagined." Dolph warned.

Jules smiled and shrugged.

"Sure, sure, I understand." Dolph continued. "You think I'm a murderer. That's just great!"

"No, you're wrong again, Dolph," Alex chimed in, "We think you had a good reason to do it, and if you finished dinner a little after seven, the three of you had plenty of time to do it."

"I think you'd both better leave."

"OK." Alex started to turn. "By the way, your receptionist thinks very highly of you. She kept saying one good thing after another about you. Aren't you married? Is something going on between you two?"

"You're finally right and nothing is going on between me and Linda." Dolph said sharply. "Now get out!"

Jules and Alex left and closed the door behind them.

"Linda," Alex smiled broadly, "my friend, Dolph, told me all about you except where you live."

"I told you before Terra Linda."

"I only think of you. Now I remember they named the town after you."

Linda smiled. "You seem to have memory problems. I hope you football playing hasn't destroyed you."

"The only problem I have right now is you. I can't stop thinking of you and all else becomes unimportant. I live in Mill Valley. That's not too far away. I'd like to take you to dinner in a super restaurant tomorrow at your convenience. OK?"

Linda's eyes questioned Alex. He didn't look as if he were lying. She hesitated then nodded.

"What time is best for you?"

"Six-thirty or seven."

"Six-thirty," he nodded. "See you tomorrow. Lucky me. Thank you."

As they headed back to the car, Jules asked, "So this whole thing was just for you to get a date with Linda?"

"That was a bonus. Made the whole trip worthwhile."

"And how does this help the case?"

"If I can get her to like and trust me, we can have multiple dates and she can tell me everything that's going on."

"I guess that's OK." Jules admitted and added, "Let's say you're right. Dolph murdered J. J. How are you going to prove it? We have no fingerprints, no computers, no laboratory—nothing. Dolph would never admit it. How the hell are you going to prove it? What evidence can we produce to bring him to trial?"

"That's for you to figure out. You're the brains. I'll get the info. You piece it together. I can do my part. You do yours. Is it a deal?"

"Sure. It's a deal. Dolph and company could have murdered J. J. You're on the right track. You take care of them with Linda's help. I've got to admit, you made a good move. If you get on the right side of Linda, she could get us a lot of good stuff."

"No problem. Don't worry. I'll get on the right side of her. I like her a lot and I haven't even really met her, but I just know I'll like her and we'll get along. I'll find out all kinds of info on Dolph and gang. What are you going to do?"

"I wish I knew. We're a team, Alex. We've got to act like a team. I'll not going to do any interviews without you. Starting right now, we are a team. Since that's the case and time is short for us, we'll lay out our plans at dinner tonight."

"OK tonight but not tomorrow night. Got a date with an angel, named Linda. See you."

Jules and Moresee jumped out of the car and rushed to the house.

DINNER

HILDA PREPARED A SIMPLE dinner of lamb chops, mashed potatoes, and green peas. It was a small square table. Hilda sat close to Jules' right, Alex across from Jules, and Charlie across from Hilda. Hilda opened a bottle of merlot wine and carefully made sure each pour was identical.

Alex wore a plain tan T shirt above his blue jeans. Jules wore a white tennis shirt and dark brown pants. Hilda wore a flowery blouse with a blue jeans skirt. Charlie wore his white Muslim robe. His two men were outside in their cars.

Jules waved a toast. Alex and Charlie waved back. Jules and Hilda touched glasses.

"After going over J. J.'s speech," Jules smiled, "I can see how just about so many could be offended. Let's go over them. His first point was that being a discriminating person was good. It meant you could recognize and appreciate differences. He then pointed out that the white race had made our current civilization of games, factories, sports, theatre, arts, roads, highways, skyscrapers, and all the other things that were absent in other societies. He claimed all were devised because the white race was lazy.

"The black race was happy to live where ever placed. He also observed that those who considered themselves 'African Americans' favored jungle-style lives while 'Black Americans' were an integral part of our civilization . He also decided that President Obama was an African-American president who's goal was to be dictator and make America a jungle. J. J. referred to Obama as the most dangerous man in America. Now, that was some of his first statement. What do you think?"

They were silent. Finally, Hilda replied, "It is impossible to pick out any one person. What J. J. said would offend everyone. The Whites are lazy. The Blacks are happy everywhere. Obama did his best to be a dictator. I guess the most offended person would be Obama, but since he accomplished so little except for new laws, he's out. If some Whites or Blacks were offended, how could we pick one particular person?"

"Obama wouldn't be the murderer," Alex spoke. "He'd send someone to do his job. Remember, he's a do nothing African American."

"So what is our decision?" Jules asked as he sipped his Merlot.

"Zero," Alex said.

"Alex is right." Charlie agreed. "We've got nothing. We're wasting our time. Take what the police decided. It was an accident. Let's forget it."

"Impossible." Jules shook his head. "He was murdered. I've got to find the murderer and then a new job."

"There's no way to find the murderer." Charlie shook his head futilely. "Give it up. You can come back with me into your old company, make a lot of money, and no problems."

Hilda held her breath as she waited for Jules' response.

"Impossible, Charlie, but thank you. My life is on a new track and I don't want to get derailed."

"Alex is right." Hilda released a deep sigh. "Thousands of people could be offended, but only a mentally disturbed person would be upset enough to murder a stranger. A lot of people could be upset or hate J. J. for what he said, but they wouldn't murder him."

"Besides," Alex chimed in, "all those who took offense with what he said are weak. Weeklings don't have the strength or courage to murder."

"So the discrimination part is devoid of suspects?" Jules asked.

"Right." Alex quickly agreed.

"It's a question mark." Charlie added.

Hilda clenched her mouth and remained silent with her doubts.

"J. J.'s next attack was on gay marriage. J. J. referred to it as a joke. What do you think about that?"

"I think it is a non-issue. J. J. said gay couples could not produce life. No one can argue with that." Hilda said.

"Gays can argue about everything and anything," Alex observed. "They feel they are special and should be treated so."

"Can you think of any gay person who'd murder J. J.?" Jules asked.

"Hell no!" Alex shook his head emphatically.

Charlie said nothing and kept his mouth firmly shut.

"And how about you, my dear?" Jules asked.

"I don't know. It's a huge, broad field, my love. Yes, someone in the previous groups could have been offended enough to murder J. J., but look at what he or she would have to have known. They'd have to have known it was Oliver's night off. They'd have to have known where Paul was and what he was doing. They'd have to have known that J. J. would open the door for them and lead them up the stairs toward his bedroom. Yes, someone in those groups could have gotten angry enough to murder, but how could we ever find the person? It's an impossible task." Jules asked, "Do you feel the same about J. J. stating that global warming, the 'Big Bang' theory, and evolution are all lies are in the same category?"

"Sure," Alex agreed. "We're wasting time. "I'm sure Dolph and gang did it. I'll prove it with Linda's help."

"How about J. J. calling Muslims killers and destroyers? What about them?" Jules asked and looked at Charlie.

"Any Muslim would have good reason to destroy someone who threw such an insult at their faith. With a billion and a half Muslims in the world, who would you chose?"

"Maybe you." Alex said with a laugh.

"Not funny!" Charlie snarled.

"No, it's not," Jules agreed. "Alex was just making one of his bad jokes, again."

Charlie kept snarling.

"Come on, Charlie. I was just kidding." Alex smiled.

Charlie's snarl remained locked in place.

"Let's get back to Dolph." Alex suggested.

"So we have these large fields of people who could be furious with what J. J. had said about them, but no way to pick out the correct murderer." Jules ignored Alex. "But we have no way to find the murderer or murderers. Right?"

"Yes, my dear."

"I know Dolph did it."

"OK," Jules agreed. "Dolph did it. What proof do you have?"

"None right now. Linda and I are going to work on it. We'll get it."

"Good. Let's suppose you've found evidence that points to Dolph being the murderer. Unless Dolph confesses, your evidence will evaporate. The police have already declared it an accident and there are no witnesses."

"So you're saying were screwed? It's a complete waste of time?"

"Not if you can get Dolph to confess willingly," Jules replied.

"Fat chance." Alex laughed. "That fits Dolph. So we're as dead as J. J.?"

"Maybe not." Jules looked hard at Hilda. "I may have something that might work." His eyes never left hers.

Hilda's lovely face watched Jules carefully.

"Since we have no way to find the killer, we'll have the killer find me. This is what I want you to do, Alex." Jules's eyes stayed on Hilda. " I want you to send an internet message to the world saying that I, Jules Cameron, know who killed J. J. and have the proof to catch him, have him convicted, and sent to prison. I want you to send that message out as soon as we finish dinner and you get home. Be sure you make it anonymous . We want him or her looking for only one person—me. Got it? Oh, and one more thing—say that I now have a witness."

"You want to see exactly what I say?"

"No, you're good at words. You'll do it good."

When dinner was finished and Alex and Charlie had left, Jules turned to Hilda, "What do you think?"

"I'm not worried about myself. I'm worried about OUR BABY. If I get killed, our baby is killed. I can't have that. It's the worst possible possibility. The next worse would you being killed. I can't have that either. That e-mail will surely kill one of us. If I weren't pregnant with our first child, I'd hope I'd be the one murdered. But I am pregnant. I'm scared—really scared. I don't see any winning scenario."

"The winning scenario is simple—the killer comes to kill me and I capture him—or her. Maybe we can't convict him—or her—for J. J.'s murder, but we can convict whoever for attempted murder on me."

"I hope it is 'attempted murder' and the 'attempt' fails. I hate to think this is the only possible way to get the murderer. Maybe it is. I hate to think that. I hate to do it. It's scary. It's dangerous."

"Yes, my dear. You are right. Don't worry about me. I'll look out for you. I'll make sure you and our baby are always safe. You can be sure of that."

"No, I can't. You've opened a new world of terrible endings."

MORNING RUN

After bringing Hilda's coffee, muffins, and newspaper, Jules put Moresee on a leash and was about to kiss Hilda good-bye.

"Wait a minute," Hilda sat up straight in bed, "you're surely not taking Moresee with you."

"He knows the trail. He'll be good company and the exercise will be good for him."

"No!" Hilda was firm. "He stays with me. I feel I need protection. Besides, I don't want you running with him on a leash. That's dangerous for both of you. I don't want you to let him off the leash as we might lose him and we'd be breaking our promise. Moresee stays with me. Have a nice run and hurry back safely, my dear Jules. Do you think it's safe for you to go?"

"Alex may not have even sent the e-mail yet. Even if he did, it's too early and no one knows where I take my run. It's safe. Don't worry." He patted Moresee on the head, took him off the leash, and left.

As he walked toward his car, he noticed a car several houses away by the sidewalk. From his experience in the drug trade, he was aware of all cars. He took his time, backed down his driveway, and started slowly down the street. The distant car was following headlights off. He couldn't help smiling. This was going to be fun. For the first time that he could remember, the police were going to be his friends. While with Charlie selling drugs, the police had been his foe. Now that he was finally an honest man, they were on the same side. That would be great dinner conversation. Charlie would be shaking his head in disbelief. Jules picked up his cell phone and called the police.

"Good-morning, Officer. I'm about to start my morning run on the fire trail off Overhill and I notice that a car is following me. I don't know who it is or why but I'm nervous. I don't want any trouble and I hope you can send an officer here quickly to find out what is going on."

The officer took Jules' name, address, and all the necessary information.

"Take your time, Mr. Cameron. You'll have help within five minutes."

Jules did take his time. Did Alex's e-mail get this rapid a response? Was he about to come face to face with J. J.'s murderer? It would have to be so. What

other reason could it be? And just think of it—the police on his side. Amazing.

Jules drove slowly up the winding road. He saw no headlights behind. That meant it was serious. He had a satisfied internal smile. They were in for a shock.

He got to the flat area and parked by the side of the road. The fire trail was about fifty yards ahead. The sun was just trying to peek over the distant hills. The other car came silently behind him, lights now on, made a "U" turn, and parked across the road about forty yards away. Jules stayed in his locked car. The followers stayed in theirs. All was still until the bright lights of another car flashed the struggling daylight. Jules got out of his car.

"What's going on here?" There were two policemen. The one speaking looked powerful and ready for action. The other was not quite as large and kept his hand close to his gun.

"I'm Jules Cameron. I was the one who called. These are the people who are following me and I don't know the reason."

The powerful one stayed close to Jules. The other with his hand twitching near his gun walked to the car.

"Get out and put your hands on top of your heads."

The driver and passenger doors opened simultaneously. The two stood still by their doors and followed instructions. The twitching hand officer walked to the car, opened the back door, and checked to make sure it was empty.

The powerful one spoke to the driver. "What's going on?"

"May I speak to you in private, officer? It's important."

"It better be. Where?"

"Just a few yards down the road."

"Go ahead. Keep your hands on top of your head." He instructed firmly the driver. "Any problem shoot his legs."

Jules couldn't be happier. Everything was working out much faster than expected. Whoever hired these thugs had to be the killer. He watched as the two walkers came to a stop about forty yards away. The driver carefully took one hand from his head, reached into his back pocket, and handed the policeman his wallet. The policeman examined it closely and the two talked for close to several minutes. The driver got a nod from the policeman and took his hands from his head. The policeman nodded to his partner and the other man lowered his hands also.

"Follow me to the police station. Any problems and you'll have severe problems."

"Am I free to take my run now, officer?" Jules asked.

"Didn't you hear me? Follow us to the station. Got It?"

"Yes, sir." Jules replied. What the hell was going on? He saw the driver of the car that had followed him, flip his car keys to his partner, and then get into the back seat of the police car. Jules shook his head. This is odd.

The police station was only a couple of miles away and they arrived quickly. The powerful one pointed to parking spots for each car. Jules obeyed.

The twitching hand policeman walked to Jules' door. "You wait here."

The two who had followed him were led into the station and didn't return to their car for about a half an hour. They got in their car and drove away.

"Your turn." The policeman opened Jules' door.

What the hell is going on? Jules thought. Something's very wrong.

Jules was led through the main office to an interrogation room where the door closed, and he sat alone. Am I suddenly the criminal?

After about a half hour, the door opened and a man dressed in a grey suit entered.

"Good-morning, Mr. Cameron. I am Doctor Stoulk. How are you feeling?"

"Just fine, doctor, and you?"

"I'm glad. Not many would be doing well after your recent experiences. It is extremely difficult to lose a loved one. You and Mr. Jackson, or J. J., as you called him had been together for a long while."

Jules almost stood up. He shook his head as if just waking. "Mr. Jackson, J. J., was my boss. I am married delightfully to my wonderful and beautiful wife, Hilda. We are about to have our first child. I couldn't be more excited."

"Of course you are." Dr. Stoulk's voice was calm and understanding as if talking to a madman. "You have been very strong. I am proud of you."

"Who were those guys who were tailing me?"

"They are detectives. They were hired to protect you."

"Who hired them?"

"A friend who knows you and is worried about you."

"And who the hell is that?"

"That's all we're allowed to tell you. They will protect you."

"From what?"

"I hear you quit the good job that your dear friend, J. J., gave you."

"That's right."

"You were rising rapidly in the company. You were growing successful and valuable to the company J. J. was very proud of you and rewarded you with gifts beyond belief. You had a good job with generous pay. You were getting increases almost every other month. Your wife is pregnant and the baby is due in a few more months. Do you think quitting your job at this time in your life was a wise thing to do?"

Jules was getting the drift. This damn doctor was a psychologist. "I guess it wasn't the smartest thing to do. I got confused."

"That's easy to do when you've lost a loved one. Let's try to put things in perspective. First, the case is closed. Mr. Jackson committed suicide. The police have examined the case thoroughly and it is now closed. He committed suicide. Maybe it was because of your marriage to Hilda. Maybe the baby coming along made it final in Mr. Jackson's mind. Regardless, he saw the end of the dear relationship between you two. It must have hurt him dreadfully."

"Oh my! I was the reason for his suicide! That makes me feel even worse."

"I understand fully. We can keep you here for a few weeks, repair you completely, and bring you back to a more normal relationship with your wife. You must try to avoid similar relationships."

"Did you have a mother and father, doctor?"

"Yes, I did."

"That's why despite all your training and studying you'll never really understand. I grew up alone. I was like a coyote surrounded by starving wolves. I was food and life to them. My life was more than different. I didn't fit in. I had to snarl and fight like hell to stay alive. J. J. gave me a cloak of steel. When any wolf tried to attack me, their teeth were cracked by my steel cloak. Finally, they left me alone. I became accepted. That's how J. J. helped me."

"A remarkable story. It makes it clear how you two became so close. I now understand and I'm here to help you. I'd like to give you another cloak of steel to help you get through the loss of your dear J. J. You must accept my new cloak."

"Yes, Doctor, I can see that now. That's wonderful, doctor. You've been a great help to me already. I'm looking forward to being repaired with your new cloak. How wonderful of those detectives following me this morning to ensure my safety. I owe my gratitude to whoever hired them. I must give them my thanks in person and reward them in some manner. Please let me know who they were and who hired them, Doctor. I must thank them. They and you have saved me. Who were they, Doctor?"

"I'm not really allowed to say anything."

"When I'm released in four weeks, I will thank you and the ones who protected me and got me into your good care. Please doctor, I have to know."

The doctor hesitated, then took out a pen and a piece of paper. "I'm sorry. I can't tell you anything." As he said this he wrote on the paper and handed it to Jules.

Jules looked at it and stuffed it in his pocket. The note read, Floss Detective Agency.

"Doctor, you've been wonderful. You have no idea how much you've helped me. Now I must go home briefly to see my pregnant wife and tell her that I'll be under your care for the next four or five weeks and when I get home I should be fully recovered. Maybe I'll even try to get my old job back. You're right.

I had a super deal. I must have been nuts to quit. I'll return as soon as possible, doctor. Thank you for your help. I feel better already."

"I don't think I can let you go now."

"You have to Doctor. Can't you see I'm the cause of one death already. I don't want my pregnant wife to contemplate or commit suicide. I would never recover. I'd be responsible for the deaths of the only two people who ever loved me. Please Doctor."

"All right, but you must return today or I'll have to have the police escort you back. Perhaps a couple should follow you now."

"Please, doctor, don't make her worries a deadly cliff. You've been great. You've helped me a lot today. I know with your help I'll get well. Thanks so much."

Jules shook his hand warmly, gave a grateful smile, and left. Damn, he thought—I'm short on time—real short. At least he had the name of the detective agency. That was a start.

He walked through the lobby looking only straight ahead. He took a deep sigh as the door closed behind him. He waited for a moment. The door stayed closed. He started to breath normally again and walked toward his car. The sun was up but the early morning air was still chilly.

The two who had followed him were standing by his car. "Hand me your phone and anything else that could record what I'm about to say. I don't want this recorded."

Jules handed it to him and waited for the important message.

"You have twenty-four hours. Either quit your investigation or your pregnant wife will be dead. There will be only one suspect—you. She'll be dead and you'll live maybe a year or two in jail, but two years would be max. Quit your investigation or that's what's going to happen for sure. It's your choice. Got it?"

"Got it."

"And don't try to tell the police. They won't believe you. They know you're a nut job." They turned and walked toward their car.

Jules watched them. As they drove away he memorized their license plate. He and Hilda would have to stay close. She must always be by his side. They would never take her. Hilda was his life. All else was decoration.

DESPERATION

As he opened the door to his home, Moresee gave him an effusive greeting. He gave short barks of joy interrupted by moans as if trying to talk. Jules gave Moresee several pats and a tug on both cheeks. Moresee calmed down but couldn't stop wagging his stubby tail. He stayed close as of on a leash.

"I'm home, dear. I have a lot to tell you." He walked in to get his breakfast on the kitchen table. Her cell phone was there, but no breakfast.

"Hilda! Hilda!" He started to walk from room to room and then ran to the last two. Moresee knew something was wrong. Jules stood still in the last room. Did she have a bad turn in her pregnancy? Had she fainted? Was she at the hospital? Every room was empty.

Then it hit him. Son of a bitch! They've got her! That's what Moresee had been trying to say. Jules remembered her phone was where his breakfast should have been. He raced to it and pressed the message button.

"Don't worry, my dear. I hope to be back soon." Her voice was calm and cold. She was in dire trouble.

Jules's legs became marshmallows. He slumped to his knees. He was dizzy. He put both hands on the carpet to keep upright. They had her. It took four minutes for his head to clear and resume standing.

NO WAY! They had gone too far. This was war. If he had to kill, he would.

Wait a minute. That wouldn't bring back Hilda. He had to find her. He had to make them talk. Dead men can't talk. He'd get them to talk. They must be outside again, watching and waiting. He hoped so.

He walked to the side window. Two guys were in a white car down the street—waiting. How interesting—different car—different color.

Now it's my turn. He went to his old-fashioned line phone and called Alex.

"They've got Hilda. Two guys got me in the police station and convinced them that I'm a nut case. Two other guys were at our home and kidnapped Hilda. I've got to get her back.

"Here's what I want you to do. There's a white car about a hundred yards short of my house. There's lots of room behind it to park. When you get here, drive as if you're out of your mind drunk. Get beside the white car and parallel park behind him. Have trouble doing it. When you get behind the car, ram it hard. I mean hard! The bigger the dent the better. When they get out, you take the guy on the passenger side. I'll take the driver. OK? Any questions?"

"Hell no. Great! I'm on my way."

Jules cracked open the front door and waited. Moresee sat patiently beside him wondering what was happening. It didn't take long. Alex's car came weaving down the narrow road. It stopped for a minute in the middle of the road, tried to make a "U" turn, acted as if confused, and started on toward Jules' house.

Alex drove past the white car, pulled into a driveway, took three tries at backing out and finally made it the fourth time. After embarrassing maneuvering, he pulled alongside the white car and stopped. Alex lay his head down on the steering wheel as if about to sleep. He shook his head violently, looked around to see where he was, and started to parallel park behind the white car. He managed not to scrape the white car, backed a good ten yards behind it, then stepped on the gas and rammed it hard.

Both men jumped out of their car. Jules opened his door and ran towards the white car's driver. Moresee happily followed. The driver was unaware of Jules. He was furious with the drunken driver. Before the driver could say a word, Jules gave him a furiously hard rabbit punch. He slumped to the ground. Jules rolled him over. He was unconscious. Jules looked over toward Alex. He had his man completely under control. The guy was also on the ground and Alex's knee was on his back.

"Empty his pockets." Jules said softly. "Everything from all his pockets."

"What the hell are you guys doing?" Alex's guy asked nervously. "Are you out of your—" He caught himself and clamped his mouth tight.

"You'll find out." Jules replied softly. Jules' guy started to recover. Jules turned him over, raised his shoulders, and gave him another firm rabbit punch. He then emptied the guy's pockets and threw the contents on the ground. Moresee inspected each piece but refrained from tasting or watering.

"Bring your guy over here, Rudy."

"Rudy?" Alex shook his head as if acting drunk again.

"That's right and don't loiter. Come on! If my guy starts to come to again, put him back to sleep. I'm going to look inside their car."

Jules took off his sweater and put all the stuff from the guy's pockets in it. He then walked to their car, opened the trunk area, and dumped the guy's goods on the left side. He went to where Alex had emptied the other guy's pockets and dumped those belongings to the right. He closed the trunk and opened the driver's door. Just what he wanted—two pair of handcuffs. He tossed them to Alex. "Put their hands behind them and load them on the back seat of your car."

"How about the sleeping guy?"

"Put him in last. If short on room, lay him on your guy's lap. Get in your car and follow me."

Jules took their car keys, put Moresee in the backseat, turned on the engine, and started slowly down the steep road. Alex followed closely.

It was a familiar ride. He did it every morning, but now it was a later than usual.

When they arrived at his morning run area, Jules parked the white car away from the regular parking area and slightly down the hill. There were five parked cars. The drivers were walking or running on the fire trail.

Jules ran over to the where the park plastic bags were to pick up dog poop, took two bags from the rack and hurried back to the white car. He opened the trunk, filled each bag with the pocket contents, and brought everything but the cell phones to Alex's car. He let Moresee out of the car, locked it, and they got in Alex's car. Moresee sat happily between Jules' knees. Jules looked at his captives.

"What the hell do you think you're doing?" Alex's guy asked. Jules' guy was shaking his head and trying to waken.

"You're Amos?" Jules asked looking at their driver's license. Alex started down the steep road.

"Yes, sir."

"And your friend's name is Winton?"

"Right again. We're your friends. We're here to help you."

"Great! Who hired you?"

"The Floss Detective Agency."

"That's who you work for. Who hired them?"

"How the hell should I know? I'm here to help Winton. I'm not a detective. Winton is. I'm just an extra body. I'm in training. Maybe he knows, but sure as hell I don't know a damn thing. We're supposed to keep you safe. Now look at me. I'm a prisoner of the guy I'm supposed to save. It took me a long time to find a job. Now I'm a dead man. Killed by the guy I'm protecting. What a mess! Damn!"

"You awake yet, Winton?" Jules asked.

"Yeah. Sort of." Winton's chin was on his chest.

"Who hired Floss Detective Agency?" Jules asked.

"Look, man, we're paid to do a job. We don't know and don't give a damn. They pay Floss. Floss pays us."

"And what were you paid to do?

"Take care of you. Keep you safe. They said you were a guy in trouble and I guess you are. Big time! You smash our car and smash us. You've got real big problems, guy. Let us go and we'll forget about what you did to our car. I'll get it

fixed, OK? We'll get back to our car and we'll follow you and keep you safe and out of trouble. Deal?"

Jules closed his eyes for a moment and had to smile internally. They've been told by the authorities, who are always right, that I'm a nut case. If I tell them I'm not, they'll laugh to themselves at the joke. Then they'll try to be kind and understanding to the poor nut case. There's no way to change their minds; so the tactics must be changed.

"You know, Winton, you're a likeable guy. Amos seems OK too. I could let you go real easy, but something's wrong. I need your help."

"What's the problem? Amos and I will try to solve it."

"I don't know where my wife is. Somehow I've lost her."

"Ah, don't worry about that." Winton sounded as sympathetic as possible. "She probably did some early morning shopping. She's probably home by now. Let's drive over and find out."

"She was kidnapped by two of your guys." Alex said sharply.

"You got problems, too?" Winton shook his head sadly. "We're in the detective business. We don't commit crimes. We solve them."

"Great!" Jules said with excitement. "But what if someone from Floss did come to our house and for one reason or another took Hilda away. Could you find out who did it and where my wife is now?"

"It didn't happen; so how can I find out something that didn't happen?"

"Couldn't you check with your office and find out who was at my house earlier?"

"Yeah, sure." Winton said with a smile. "Give me my phone."

"You aren't the guys who took me to the police station this morning. What's the deal?"

"No, Mr. Cameron, we were assigned to you at eight this morning. This is a new job for us. It was a trial case. I guess we flunked." Winton's voice was soft, kind and trying to sound understanding.

"Then how come, Mr. Cameron," Alex broke in, "your wife, Hilda, has been kidnapped from your home?"

"Look, Rudy, stay out of this." Jules said sharply.

"But—"

"No 'buts,' Rudy. They're here to help us. Maybe Hilda did just leave for a moment."

"That's not so, Jules," Alex liked the game, "you called me early this morning and told me she had been kidnapped. We thought these were the guys that did it. That's why we bumped their car and kidnapped them. Now we can exchange them for her. It's a good deal—two for one."

"Yeah, Rudy, that's great." Jules said with enthusiasm. "We can exchange two for one—my wife, Hilda. That's a great deal for everyone. So where's my wife?"

"Give us our phones," Winton said softly and kindly, "and we'll find out."

"Your phones are back in your car. You got some 'throw aways,' Rudy?"

"Yeah sure as usual. Three today. How many?"

"Just one. No funny stuff." Jules took the phone and handed it to Winton.

Winton held it as if it were about to explode. "What do you want me to say?"

"Just who you are and then hand the phone to me. Got it?"

Winton nodded and dialed. He told the receptionist who he was and handed the phone immediately to Jules.

"We've been worried about you and Amos. Let me connect you with Mr. Engals. Just a minute, please."

The phone rang twice and was picked up.

"Mr. Engals, I have Winton on the line." The receptionist said.

"Where the hell have you been? Why haven't you answered our calls? Are you and Amos OK?"

"They're both OK, Mr. Engals. This is Jules Cameron speaking."

"Well, Mr. Cameron, what the hell do you think you're doing?"

"First of all, don't bother trying to track this call. It's not traceable. Secondly, where is my wife? I'll trade your two boys for her. Is it a deal?"

"Look, Cameron, you're in serious trouble. You have kidnapped two of my detectives. This is serious. You'll go to jail for a long time."

"I just want a trade. You kidnapped my wife. I took your two boys in exchange. You did the kidnapping. I'm just making an exchange."

"Mr. Cameron, please try to understand. We did not kidnap your wife. We are protecting her from a husband who is mentally insecure. Your actions and words show how mentally disturbed you are and how important it is to protect your wife from you."

Jules shook his head, hung up, and tossed the phone out the window. "Hand me another one." He put his hand out toward Alex.

"I only have one left after this one." Alex gave the phone to Jules.

Jules dialed another number. "Hey man, no dinner tonight. They've got Hilda."

"What the hell are you talking about? Who has Hilda?" Charlie asked.

"You know Floss Detective Agency?"

"Hell yes! Got a couple of good customers there. Hey, why don't you come here for dinner? It's my turn anyway."

"I've got a friend, two prisoners from Floss, and a dog. Can you handle that?"

"Hell yes! I'll put your prisoners in our dungeon. Hurry! I've got to hear this. I'll have a couple of Muslims at our street to guide you. Blindfold them."

Jules hung up and handed the phone to Alex. "Pull over Rudy. I'll drive."

"Need another phone? It's my last one."

"Save it. Cover their eyes."

NEW PLANS

As Jules drove across the Golden Gate Bridge to San Francisco, he asked, "Do you have a wife and any kids, Winton?"

"Yeah, a great wife and two great kids. A boy and a girl. My little girl is only three."

"And your boy?"

"He'll be seven next month. They're going to worry like hell about me. Let us go and I'll check all about your Hilda at the office. I'll send you the info."

"That must be great to have a wife and two kids." Jules mused.

"You have a wife, Jules." Alex had to get in the game. "Remember? Hilda is pregnant and you're going to have your first child shortly."

"Oh my! That's right." Jules rubbed his forehead. "I have a wife and my first kid is on the way. I just don't know where I put her. How about you, Amos? You got a wife and kids, too?"

"No. Just me. You're killing me."

"How about this for a deal, guys?" he asked. "You get us Hilda, you go home, we go home, everyone's happy. Is that OK with you, Jules?"

"Almost." Jules's voice became stern and precise. "I also need to know who hired Floss Detective Agency. I just need two things. Hilda is number one. The name of you client is number two. I need them both. Any questions?"

"Maybe she went out to do some shopping or see a friend or something." Amos suggested. "She may is doing a favor for you or maybe she had to see a doctor and the baby is coming early."

"Forget it, Amos." Jules was finished with games. "My wife, Hilda, was kidnapped this morning. When I was at the police station and they labeled me 'nuts,' some guys went to my house and kidnapped Hilda. I want her back safe and without one scratch or mark on her and I want the name of your client. When I have that, you're free. Got it?"

"You guys are in a lot of trouble." Winton's voice had a bit of a tremble in it. "Let us out now. Take off the cuffs. Throw me the keys. We'll walk back to our car and never say a word or turn you in. You'll both go to jail for a long time for what you're both doing. Kidnapping is serious."

"How about Moresee?" Alex asked.

"What? Who?"

"He's the guy who planned all this." Alex smiled at his own joke.

"That's right." Jules said. "Kidnapping is real serious. You were the ones who started this. If my wife dies, so will both of you. Murder is even more serious. How big is Floss?"

"They're the largest in the state."

"Interesting. So they're expensive. Someone is spending a lot of money. How fast can you find out for me, Winton?"

"I don't know."

"Your wife and kids are really going to be worried. I've got to know, Winton. You're with me until I find out."

"Look, Mr. Cameron, have a heart. If I find that out for you, I'll be fired. I need my job; so does Amos."

"Let's try this. I want you both to be able to go home. Here's something you can do. Tell me who was supposedly protecting me early this morning before you came. What were their names?"

"I don't know. We thought we were the first and only."

"You're not. There were two before you. What were their names and addresses? Also, I want the names and addresses of the guys who went to my house when I was out to take my morning run. Can you do that?"

"Sure, sure." Winton said quickly. "Unlock my hands and give me some paper and a pen or pencil."

Jules smiled to himself. They still think they're dealing with a mad man. There's only one course to take—act like a mad man.

"Hey, Rudy, you getting bored?"

"Damn right. All talk and no action."

"How about if I untie Amos and you two have a match?"

"He's pretty small. He'd be too easy. How about Winton? He's a lot bigger."

"How about it, Winton?" Jules asked. "But I've got to warn you. If you start winning, I'll put a bullet in your left leg."

"He doesn't have a chance." Alex shook his head. "How bad can I hurt him?"

"Don't kill him and no hospital bills. Are you ready, Winton?"

"Come on now guys. Ease off. We're going the wrong direction. I want to help. I really do."

"Then it's real simple." Jules smiled.

"Call your office and ask who took my wife and where did they take her. Also, you can tell them that you two will be free when she is. Deal?"

"What if your wife has not been kidnapped and she's just out shopping or something? They'll think I'm nuts—like you—and any info I get will be a joke."

"I guess it's time for our fight. You ready, Rudy?"

Alex hunched his shoulders. "Damn right. Where we going to do it? I

know a nice lonely spot in the woods. I'll take his cuffs of there. No one will hear the screams. This should be fun."

"Hold on for just a minute." Jules open the car door and walked far enough away not to be heard before dialing. "Hey, Charlie, we're on our way."

"How many?"

"Four and our dog."

"Blindfold the Floss guys, keep them and your dog in the car. OK?"

"Sure. Be there shortly."

DINNER AT CHARLIE'S

"You got the wrong street." Alex looked at the two Muslims directing them.

"No, I don't. Now you know why these guys had to be blindfolded."

"Got it! I forgot about last night. What a surprise!"

"He's a new man. Lucky for us." Jules nodded.

The two men in Muslim attire directed them to a parking area. One of the Muslims raised his hand and they stopped. One opened the driver's side and the other where Alex was sitting. As Jules and Alex got out the Muslim men then reached in and pulled out handcuffed and blindfolded Amos and Winton.

"We'll take care of them. Go to the fifth floor."

"Hey, wait a minute!" Winton nervously tried to shout. "What the hell's going on? Let us go! What do you want? Tell me and it's yours. Come on, Jules! Let us go!"

"No problem." Jules replied in a soft, kind voice. "Number one—where is my dear wife, Hilda. Number two—who hired Floss? Tell me that and you're free."

"We don't know. Honest Jules—we don't know. Come on—let us go."

"Just be patient. You know I'm a little nuts. I'm sure you'll be comfortable."

As one led Amos and Winton away, the other whispered to Jules, "Fourth floor—not the fifth—the fourth."

Jules nodded. "What about the car? Just leave it here?"

"Hey, Jules, I've got my big date tonight you know with—"

"That's right you're going to Terra Linda. Great! Find out what you can. The car is yours. Good-luck. We need answers."

"I'll get them. How about you?"

"I'll be OK. Go on! Let me know what you find out. I've got to get Hilda. I've got to!" He flipped the car keys to Alex

"Don't worry. I'll get the answers. I'm sure of it."

With that, Alex got in his car, had a difficult time turning around in the narrow alley, and drove away.

Fourth floor, Jules mused. What the hell difference did it make? The guys were blindfolded and Charlie owned the whole damn run-down building.

Jules entered the old building. It was a mess with cracks in the ceiling, walls, and flooring and the smell of unkempt old age. He entered an open elevator with only a chain in front of it. Jules got in, looked at the fifth button, wanted to push it, but pushed fourth as instructed.

It was not a quiet elevator. It was slow and noisy. Since Charlie had removed portions of the inside stairs, Charlie could always hear people coming and be well prepared. The elevator made its painful journey to the fourth floor. Jules stood by the open elevator door. As it started to pass the fourth floor, Jules saw a long white robes that covered the shoes. The robe covered arms came into view with only the fingers of the black hands visible. Jules kept his eyes straight ahead and watched the mystery unfold. He came to the face. It was Charlie with his Muslim headgear. Jules laughed.

"You look great, Charlie. Your new attire still gets me."

"It's for guys who like to win. Come on in! Look around."

Jules did with amazement. It was all done in Muslim furnishings and style—simple, clean, new, and expensive. Jules shook his head in amazement. "I don't get it, Charlie. What happened to the penthouse?"

"That's my English housing." Charlie faked an aristocratic English accent.

"So are you Muslim, English, or American?"

"Yes."

"Go on—enlighten me."

"When I'm a Muslim, I become invisible to the police. When I'm English, I'm respected. When I'm an American, I have to be very careful all the time. When I or my employees, shall we say, go to work, we're Muslims. I'm sure we could sell our drugs in the middle of the street and not get arrested, but we don't. We don't want to embarrass the police. They are our friends. We're making a fortune now, buddy. Want to rejoin us?"

"Thanks, but no thanks. I've got enough problems. But how do the real Muslims let you get away with this?"

"It's simple. I give them a big percentage of what comes in, I tell them I'm one of them, and they take care of me. I've got a lot coming in now—a lot. Hey, you mentioned Hilda is gone. Come on, sit down. What the hell happened?"

Jules explained how he was sure this was an effort by J. J.'s murderer to avoid detection. Someone had a lot of money to hire the Floss Detective Agency. He went on to list those he thought had reason to murder J. J. It was a long list. The final steps had been this morning when he called the police to tell them he was being followed so he could take his morning run. He turned out to be the bad guy—a nut case—who was going to be locked up in a physiatric ward indefinitely.

He told how he had managed to let his doctor let him go home to tell his pregnant wife, and how he was to return shortly. The whole thing was a complete mess. He had lost J. J. Now he had lost Hilda. If she were in any trouble, this could cause serious trouble to the pregnancy and Hilda. Saving her would save him and their soon to be child. He had to save her quickly. Nothing was more important to her, to him, to their baby.

Charlie listened, smiled, and shook his head. "So the smartest guy in school is now a first class nut case. I told you, you were pushing your brain too hard, but you never listen to me. So what do you want for dinner?"

"After I tell you all this you want to talk about food?"

"Hell yes. Why not? What do you want first—Hilda or J. J.'s murderer? You want it before or after dinner?"

"You know, Charlie, I'm not in the mood to laugh. Hilda is my life. I'm dead without her. I'll worry myself to death. She's that important."

"No problem. I can get her to you in probably less than an hour."

"Great! Let's do it."

"All you have to do is become a Muslim. I'll tell the guys in charge. They'll go to Floss, scare the hell out of them, and Hilda will be back in your home and arms before we finish dinner."

"So all I have to do is say I'm a Muslim?"

"No, you have to become one—like me. It doesn't hurt at all. You'll like it."

Jules thought for a moment then shook his head. "Hell, Charlie, I'm not selling drugs anymore. I've become an honest man. I can't pretend I'm a Muslim."

"Then don't pretend. Become one. Save Hilda and your baby."

"Then I become a Muslim and when we're rejoined, she has to become a Muslim and our baby, too. I can't do that to them. I know Hilda. She'd reject that and be furious with me. I can't, Charlie."

"It's your decision."

"OK, Charlie, you're now a happy Muslim. I hope you know that if you ever become an unhappy Muslim and leave, that is reason for them to kill you. Now that you've joined, you can't leave alive."

"How quickly you forget! I break all laws. Why should Muslim laws be any different? Shit, Jules, I'm getting up close to the big bucks one percenters. I'm making more money breaking the law than the ninety-nine percent below me who're trying to follow the thousands of laws floating down like a giant net which will tie them up and steal their money. The net throwers will laugh and have fun. The broke ninety-nine percenters will keep moving on like zombies."

"That net is a lot more friendly than a steel knife in your heart, Charlie."

"You still don't get it. There are three levels of society now. Muslims are number one. Government workers are number two. Everyone else is number zero. I used to be afraid of the police. Now they're afraid of me. They almost bow down to me. I'm a Muslim. I am in charge. Why? Because Obama is a Muslim and he made it this way."

"Since you're a Muslim, why can't you tell the big guys that you have a friend who wants his wife back. Can't they do that?"

"Sure, there's only one problem—they won't do a damn thing for a Christian. You're shit, Jules, and they won't dirty their hands on you. Come on! Join us. It won't hurt a bit. You'll have Hilda back and you'll have the Muslims backing you. All the other religions are pussies."

"Well, let's see, Charlie. OK I become a Muslim. Now I'm under Shira Law. I guess I could tell Hilda 'I divorce you' and that's that. She's divorced. No legal expense or problems. Now there's a great deal! The problem is I could never divorce her. But if she has to wear a burka, keep her face and figured covered, and be my convenience, she might divorce me, but then again, under Shira law is the wife allowed to divorce the husband? I doubt it. It's a one-way street designed only for the man. If I were to become a Muslim, Hilda will become in essence my slave. Impossible. That would ruin her life and mine. If I were single, I couldn't do it. The Muslims don't think the same as us. No way! Now what, Charlie?"

"You're not very tolerant. In fact, you're miserably intolerant. What do you think of that?"

"I think you're absolutely right. You know what tolerance is? It's weakness. It is surrender. The bad deed wins and you lose. The bad deed becomes accepted and then becomes right. If you tolerate a crime, that crime converts into being OK. That's stupid! If someone commits a crime, punish them. Don't tolerate and excuse it. Punish it. Let the punishment fit the crime. When you tolerate evil, as time passes the evil become acceptable and then OK. If you object, you become the one who's wrong. That's how our society got so screwed up. Bad deeds have become tolerated. Right and wrong have vanished. Those who object are bigots or worse."

"You sound like a young J. J. You've been brainwashed."

"You're probably right. Certain things he said keep shouting in my mind like; 'If you unlock your front door and blithely sweep out right and wrong, the hurricane of chaos will storm in to your ruin.' To me, tolerance is the broom sweeping out right and wrong."

"You'd make a perfect Muslim. Right and wrong are clear and they don't tolerate a damn thing. Come on! Join us. You'll be at the top of the heap instead of the gravel everyone steps on. Come on! Give it a try!"

"I'm an American. I'm proud of it. I can't do it to myself and there's no way in heaven or hell I could do that to Hilda. No, Charlie, forget it."

"OK, as I said before, let's have dinner and talk it over. What do you want—fish or steak?"

"Steak."

Charlie clapped his hands and two black Muslims hurried into the room. Charlie placed the order and they left just as quickly.

Charlie and Jules gave each other a silent toast with their red wine as they started their dinners.

"So basically, Charlie, there's nothing you can do."

"I didn't say that. There's nothing I can do as a Muslim, but maybe I can help as a friend. I have a couple of customers at Floss. One is taking the big stuff. I'll see what I can get from him."

"When?"

"I'll call him after dinner."

"I'm finished." Jules replied.

"Come on, Jules! Give me a break. I'm not going to call him until you actually finish your dinner. Do you understand, my naughty little boy?"

"Yes, mother. Whatever you say."

As soon as they finished dinner, Charlie pulled out his cell phone and dialed.

HELP ON THE WAY

"Hey, Bingo, it's me—Charlie. I've got a good deal for you. I've got some super stuff. It's the best. I put aside some especially for you. It's really unbelievable."

Momentary silence. Charlie gave a short laugh.

"No, no, Bingo—not that. It's from Venezuela and it's better than any woman in the world. You take one swallow and you're on your way to Mars and beyond in your own rocket ship. And you know what the good thing is? It's free, if you can do one simple thing for me. What do you say?"

Momentary silence. Charlie continued.

"Floss picked up the wife of a guy I knew in high school, Hilda Cameron. Tell me where she is and you're going to get the ride you've dreamed of—free!"

There was a long silence.

"Sure I know him. As I told you, I went to high school with him. I haven't seen him in years. I have no idea where he is—probably at his home. He knows I have a lot of friends and called me. He thought Floss was involved. What do you say? You want the good stuff? You give me something. You'll be rewarded. You'll get the best. What do you say?"

Momentary silence.

"Yeah, sure, I'll turn on the TV and whatever it is, I'll split it with you fifty-fifty. Now tell me where Hilda is."

Momentary silence.

"OK, thanks, Bingo. You're going to get the ride of your life. Yeah, I'm turning it on right now." With this Charlie hung up and turned on the TV which was hidden in a distant corner of the room.

Jules Hs been listening and watching Charlie. His eyes then followed Charlie's eyes to the TV. Below the show on the screen was a continuous message.

"Jules Cameron has escaped from the Mill Valley jail. He is mentally unstable and dangerous. A hundred-thousand-dollar reward is offered for his capture."

"Hey, I always thought you were only worth a couple of bucks. One hundred grand! Wow! I'm proud of you."

"Where's Hilda?"

"She's in the penthouse at the top of the Floss Building. I've seen it. It's fantastic! You'd think you were in a palace or something. You have everything you'd ever want at your fingertips. She's a lucky gal."

"Bullshit! She's my wife. All her thoughts are centered on our first child. This is the worst torture possible for her. She and our baby are in solitary confinement. There's no way she can be happy. She is life and filled with new life. I've got to get her out of there. Damn it! I have to!"

"Come on, Jules, be realistic. OK, she's alone. I'll grant you that, but she's in a super safe spot. You don't have to worry about her safety."

"Her physical safety is good. Her mental and emotional safety is in jeopardy and so for her health and that of our baby's, I've got to get her out of there fast."

"You got any sweet thoughts of how to do it?"

"Not yet, but I will. Someone's got one hell of a lot of money to throw around. Whoever is putting up that much dough is guilty as hell for the murder of J. J. I've got him real worried."

"Big deal, Jules. How you gonna get him? So you find him and accuse him. You know who's gonna be tossed behind the steel bars? You! There's only one thing you can do—leave the country. Get out fast or you'll be in a real prison and not the super kind Hilda's in."

"Impossible! How loyal are your guys? I see some of the old gang are still with you, but how about the new guys. Would they sell me out for a hundred grand?"

"Shit man! I would. Sure as hell one or more would. You got to get out of here fast, man."

Jules slapped his right knee hard and then his forehead. "Saccharine!"

"Oh shit! You finally have a sweet idea."

"If I were to change my clothes and wore a Muslim robe, would they turn in a brother Muslim?"

"Shit man! Just a few seconds ago you told me it was impossible for you to be a Muslim. Now you want to join us?"

"I'm not going to be a Muslim. I'm just going to look like one. The game's called Masquerade. That will make me invisible to the world. Would your guys turn in a fellow Muslim?"

"Of course not unless they wanted to die. Why the sudden change?"

"Call your customer back at Floss and tell him that you and Mohamad Moresee need to see the big guy at Floss tomorrow morning early. It's super important. Call him right now."

"Now you're Mohamed?" Charlie shook his head with a smile. What was the game? He picked up his phone and dialed Bingo.

"Hey, Bingo, Mohamed Moresee and I need to talk to the head man at Floss tomorrow first thing. Tell him it's super important."

Momentary silence.

"I can't tell you the reason, Bingo. Just tell him that me and one of our most important guys, Mohammed Moresee, need to see him as quickly as possible. He's probably not there now so call him at home and tell him. It's that important." With that Charlie hung up.

Jules and Charlie sat quietly. They watched the phone as if worried it would explode. There were four minutes of silence and then it rang.

"Bingo?" Charlie asked.

Momentary silence.

"Good! Eight-thirty is fine." He hung up and turned to Jules. "OK?"

Jules nodded approval. "Perfect! Got a place for me to sleep? Got a robe for me? I need a heavy beard—real heavy—and something to darken my skin. OK?"

"No problem, but what the hell is going on?"

"I want to become invisible. You are right. The Muslims are on the top of the heap of leaves. The citizens of America are the rotting leaves on the bottom. I'll put on Muslim attire, darken my face, and put on a dark, black, beard. I'll look like a religious guy. No one will dare question me. I'll be on the top of the heap with you guys. I'll be a feared and sacred Muslim. The ex-President of the United States will be on my side. I'll have his backing. You've convinced me, Charlie. Now how safe will I be with your guys?"

"You'll be part of our team again, Jules old chum. They'll protect you. They'll think something big is in the works and they'll want to be part of it. You'll be safe with us. But I don't understand. I offered you to be a Muslim before. You spit in my face. Now you want to dress up like a kingpin. What's the deal?"

"It's a game. People go to parties all the time dressed to fool others. It's just a temporary thing. It's party clothes. It's a game."

"I hope we both win this scary game."

"Got a room where I can sleep?"

"A whole damn floor."

"Good. Is it OK to have Moresee join me?"

"Hell yes. You're going to owe me big time. Want to be partners again? I could use you."

"Who knows? Working with you would be a lot better than being in the idiot tank—no, that's wrong. It would be slightly better." Jules smiled.

"Thanks a lot, buddy. What the hell was the 'saccharine'? I know you had a sweet thought. What's the deal?"

"I still have things to work out in my mind. I'm going to take Moresee for a walk, buy him some food, and then we'll be back. OK? Wait a minute—what did your guys do with Moresee?"

"I'm sure he's in with your two hostages."

Jules shook his head and smiled. "I forgot about them. Have your men drive them down to Market Street and release them. I don't need them anymore. They'll be happy and there'll be one less problem."

Charlie lifted his shoulders with wonder. "If you say so, Mohamed. OK"

"Now let's play masquerade. Get me a robe and call in your guy to fix me up. He's got to do a good job. I want to look important."

"What are you going to wear under your robes?"

"Regular clothes. It's a masquerade."

"Polished brown dress shoes with your slacks showing as you walk? That's no masquerade. That's a dead deal,"

"Oh hell, loan me a pair of your 'fits the world' slippers. Have someone fix up my face."

Charlie walked near the window and pulled cord four times. A man sneaked into the room as if guilty of some crime. Charlie pointed to Jules and the transformation started.

"Put lots of hair on my face." Jules instructed, and Joshua nodded.

THE WALK

IT TOOK ALMOST TWO hours to fix up Jules' face, hands, feet, and even his eyebrows and hair. The white robe with red strips was easy to wear. Jules changed his shoes for slippers and rolled up his pant legs close to his knees. As the work was being completed, Moresee was brought into the room.

Moresee wanted to run to Jules, but the leash held him. Charlie took the leash and pulled Moresee to him. Moresee obeyed and sat down by Charlie but he couldn't take his eyes off Jules. He was anxiously waiting for the time he could race to him and feel at home.

"He's an OK dog." Charlie gently patted Moresee on the head. "You know Muslims don't like dogs. If you walk with him, you may be undressing yourself."

"Only to Muslims. Everyone else will be blind on their cell phones, have radio cables in their ears, or rushing somewhere. They're electronically blind."

Joshua stepped back and looked at his art. "Done."

"Go look in the full length mirror on the back of the door," Charlie suggested.

Jules adjusted his robe and walked over to Moresee who was wagging his entire back with anticipation. He took the leash from Charlie and Moresee was about to jump onto Jules' robe.

"No, no, my good boy. Down. You stay down." He grabbed Moresee's collar and pulled him close. "You've been good. We're going to go now." He turned to Charlie. "We'll be back shortly."

"Will you then tell me the sweet news?"

"Tomorrow at breakfast. You'll get the whole plan. By the way, which floor is our room?"

"You'll find out tomorrow at breakfast."

Jules shook his head scornfully.

"OK," Charlie put his hands on his hips, "the second floor is all yours."

"What about a car?"

"Can't you walk him on the street? Come on! He's a spoiled brat."

"Right again."

"You're one miserable guest. If Hilda wasn't such a damn good cook, I'd tell you to go to hell. Since she is, go on down. It'll be ready for you."

"Thank you, stomach. I mean Charlie." Jules then turned to Joshua. "Will everything be OK by tomorrow?"

"Don't wash or shave."

"I'll stink."

"Don't wash or shave."

Jules took Moresee over to the mirror behind the door and looked at himself. He was a completely different man. He didn't recognize himself. "Sensational!" He nodded to his transformer.

He nodded back with a smile.

Jules opened the door and they went into the open elevator. It would be dark shortly. He knew the best solitary place for the walk.

Two robed Muslims were standing by a grey Dodge pick-up. One handed him the keys and the other opened the door for him. Jules lifted Moresee into the driver's seat, pushed him to the passenger side, and then climbed in.

Before turning the key, he looked at Moresee who was looking through the windshield, panting, and smiling. Jules had to pat his head. "You're a good boy, Moresee. You're about all I have now. Mind if I just call you 'More'?"

Moresee kept smiling and looking straight ahead. Jules kept him company with his own smile.

Jules drove to Geary Street and continued straight West until he came to the Great Highway which was a narrow street alongside the

Pacific Ocean. Many times, the Spring winds would make it impassable with the heavy winds moving the sand dunes onto the narrow road. This evening the road was clear. He continued up a hill. To his left was the famed Olympic Club golf course. Almost directly across from it was a walking area on a wild sandy area above the beach. Jules drove in and parked. He put Moresee's leash in his back pocket and opened the passenger's door for Moresee who jumped out with pleasure and excitement.

The few cars still there were being loaded with for all to go home.

"We'll be alone shortly." Jules advised Moresee as they walked across the sandy plane aimlessly.

It was almost dark. A cold fog bank was moving in. It covered the faint light from the moon. Jules could barely see the path they were on. After about a half an hour, Jules sat down on a small dune.

"You know, More, hey, your new name is perfect. You know More than me. I'm just stumbling along. You're a good boy." Moresee was panting happily and lay down beside his new master.

"I've got a problem—no, no, forgive me. We have a problem, my good More. In fact, we have more of a problem, More, than I imagined. It seems you've become the emphasis in my life. I'll tell you more, More, and maybe you can solve mu dilemma. Don't take it hard if you can't. It's OK.

"We can free your mother, Saint Hilda. No problem. She'll be at home with you and you'll both be sort of happy. There'll be one piece of the puzzle missing—me. How the hell do I prove to the world I'm not insane?

"If I can't, I'll never join you two. Look at this picture, my good boy. Maybe I'm God. I was born apparently without parents. I finally find someone I accept as my father. He teaches me business, right and wrong, and all the little things in life to make it fun and sensible. He is taken away from me by murder. I finally find the wonderful woman who completely fills the empty hole my mother should have filled. That hole is now completely filled and overflowing. Now she is taken away from me because they say I'm nuts. I am a danger to her. How can I ever be with her? How can I prove my sanity to experts who are never wrong and will prove it with fictional facts and figures? What is the special piece I need to win? I wish I could say "saccharine," but I can't." Jules got up to go to their car.

He suddenly realized he had no idea of the correct direction. He had wandered away aimlessly. Now they were lost in the endless sand and dark. A car's horn saved them. There was one road and one ocean. They headed for the car noise. When they reached the road, they were on the side of a hill. They walked up the hill to the parking area.

There was no trouble finding their car. It was the only one left. Jules lifted More onto the driver's seat. More moved quickly to the passenger seat. Jules shook his head, smiled, and gave More a pat on his head and a pinch on his cheek.

"Why can't people be more like, you More? OK, maybe I am nuts. You don't give a damn. You accept me and are loyal to me. You are wonderful. In fact, you are getting More and More wonderful every passing second." With this, Jules smiled momentarily at his humor. He put the key in the ignition, and then it hit him.

He slapped his knee with his fist. "Damn it Jules! You're a cry baby. You're crying on your own shoulders. Oh, poor darling! What you've been through! Yes, what the hell have you been through? What have you solved? Not a damn thing. OK, Hilda will be home tomorrow, but where will you be? Who put up a hundred grand to ruin you? One of J. J.'s opponents in the Senate race? You don't know. You don't know a damn thing. Stop your crying! Get with it."

SAVING HILDA

NEITHER JULES NOR CHARLIE were aware of what they were eating at breakfast. Jules was explaining in exact detail his plan. Charlie was amazed, kept nodding, and doing his best to memorize and keep it in logical order. Of course it would work. How come he hadn't seen it? It was simple and obvious.

Charlie was instructed to do all the talking because Jules, Mohamed Moresee, had just had a throat operation and could barely whisper. Any advice or instructions Jules would whisper into Charlies' ear. Floss would be recording everything but they would not get Jules' voice. He would remain the mysterious Muslim. Charlie brought two of his biggest guys dressed in Muslim attire with them—just in case.

The Floss Detective Agency building was one of the new skyscrapers in San Francisco. It was fifteen stories high and rose on a small hill overlooking the bay. The agency had the top five floors and the rest were rented to various companies. The lobby's floor, wall, and ceiling sparkled with its shiny newness. The four men entered the elevator and pressed the button that read, "FLOSS." It was the tenth floor. Jules glanced at his wristwatch. It was eight-seventeen.

The receptionist was petite and attractive. Alex would love her, Jules thought and then wondered what had happened on Alex's date with Linda last night. He was sure Alex would drop by later and tell all.

The receptionist led them into the office. On a huge desk that almost curved completely around him in a semicircle was a sign reading "Melvin R. Floss, Jr." Melvin was seated and had no intention of rising to meet them. He had grey hair, looked to be in his mid-sixties, wore a scowl and a dominating attitude. Standing behind him was a tall, skinny man with dark hair, dark clothes, and dark mean face.

Charlie walked into the room first followed by his two men supporting Jules.

"I am Mr. Floss, and this is my assistant, Jerold Black. What do you want?" Melvin asked sharply from his stuffed chair. He did not suggest they sit. It was not a welcome. It was a challenge.

"We want you to feel comfortable, Mr. Floss and not have any worries about us." Charlie started taking his pistols, money, an everything else out of his robe and placing them neatly in a pile on the floor. "Do the same" he nodded to his men. "Empty everything out of your pockets and put everything, and I mean everything, neatly on the rug. Mohamad Moresee does not understand English yet so help him also." Charlie nodded to one of the men supporting Jules. That man spoke Arabic to Jules who nodded, didn't understand one word, but took everything out of his robe except for his recorder which he kept neatly tucked under his left arm.

Melvin's eyes became locked on the guns. They grew wide with worry. Jerold's face got so dark his eyes had to squint to see. Melvin looked at the separate piles of money, credit cards and pistols and almost shouted, "What the hell is going on? Who are you?"

Jules motioned to Charlie. He came and Jules whispered in his ear. Jules whispered back.

"We want Hilda Cameron." Charlie said in a calm, certain voice. "She is ours. She belongs to us, but I don't want you to worry. We came in peace. We're here to make a peaceful deal. We want to share a hundred grand with you. We know how to get it and we'll split it with you. Fifty grand for us. Fifty grand for you. How about it?" Charlie asked.

"First of all, who the hell are you?"

"Charlie is all you need to know. I like money and I'm sure you do, too. How about it?"

"I run a well-respected and honorable company. I will never do anything illegal. Maybe it's time for you to pick up your guns and leave."

"Everything is legal. You have nothing to worry about. Mohamad Moresee just came into our country by way of Mexico for one reason—destroy Jules Cameron. He is a danger and a threat. We saw on the news that they are offering a hundred grand for his capture. Mohamad knows how to get him. Interested?"

"Do you intend to shoot and kill him?" Melvin asked with a scowl.

"Not necessarily—not unless he tries to kill us. He's a mental case, you know."

"Forget the guns. Get rid of them. I'll have nothing to do with any amount of money with any type of crime especially murder."

"But he's a mental case," Charlie persisted. "What if he tries to kill one of us?"

"He's not a mental case. Forget that. We made the police believe that just to get him out of the way. Now what's your deal?"

Jules could have let out a loud scream of delight. He was clear and it was recorded. Thank you, thank you, Charlie. Hooray!

"It's very simple. That Cameron guy loves Hilda, his wife. You've got her locked up here."

"No, we don't. Who told you that?"

"Yes, you do." Charlie shot back. "I can get any information I want. I've got many friends everywhere. I've been told she's locked up in the penthouse; so she is. That Jules guy can't get to her; so you'll never catch him. But—if you set her free and let her go back to her home, sure as hell that Jules guy will somehow try to see her. If you have your men around waiting and watching, he'll see them and you'll still never catch him. If you let us take her to her home, we'll be her friends and saviors. Jules will feel safe and show up. We'll catch him, turn him over to you, and we'll split the hundred grand. How about it?"

"I'm still worried about your guns. I don't want any murder to happen for any reason. There is no reason to kill him. He's not a mental case."

"Guaranteed. No guns. No problems. No murders. You'll get him clean."

"How can I trust you? Who is Mohamad and where is he from?"

"He said outside of a town called Dhaka in Bangladesh, wherever that is. I don't know. He had a throat operation back there. That's why he can't talk. That's probably good. I have trouble understanding him. He'd have to say everything a million times for you to understand. He's the guy who wants Cameron caught. He's read all about Cameron's boss and the things Cameron has said against the Muslims. Mohamad is furious."

"What the hell are you talking about?" Melvin shook his head. "I haven't read anything about Cameron talking negative about the Muslims."

"I guess it's in all their papers back there. They really hate him."

"And what is your proposal?"

"We take Hilda gal back to her home. Your guys stay away. We'll be her friends. The Cameron guy needs his wife. We know that. He'll show up sometime

for sure to see her. Our men will capture him and bring him to you. You can then bring him to the police and collect the hundred grand reward. My only question is—will you remember me or will you keep all for yourself?"

"I know you're not used to dealing with honorable people. My word is sacred. I do not cheat people. You bring Cameron here and you'll get your fifty thousand dollar reward. Count on it."

"I don't trust many people. Somehow everyone I know thinks only about their own benefits—never about mine. You, I'll trust."

"It's a deal. I'll have my men drive her back to her home."

"No, you can't do that. If the Cameron guy sees or a friend of his see they'll know it's a set-up. We have to be the good guys. We have to drive her to her house. We have to look out for her and capture, not kill, Cameron."

Melvin thought it over for a bit, nodded, and said, "I'll have her brought down."

"Just a minute." Dark Jerrold interrupted. "Tomorrow is J. J.'s funeral. Cameron will definitely show up for that. We'll capture him there and that closes the other deal."

"That's right." Melvin nodded and smiled. "If he's at the funeral tomorrow, we'll catch him and this other deal is off, correct?"

"Sure, but if he knew the funeral was tomorrow—" Charlie caught himself. "How could he know?"

"Because he's smart. He's smarter than the police. Why do you think they put that ad on TV? They can't find him. He's a super smart guy. If he's at the funeral tomorrow and we catch him, your deal is off, right?"

Jules was basking in the information. You're doing great, Charlie. I'm a sane man again. Thank you, thank you, thank you.

"Yeah, of course. You catch him—no deal. I catch him and bring him to you we split a hundred grand fifty—fifty. Deal?"

"How can we be sure you won't bring Jules to the police and keep the entire one hundred thousand dollars for yourself?" Dark Jerold asked.

"I do not—never—go to the police." Charlie replied. "Shall we say they are not my friends. Do you understand? Deal or no deal?"

"Agreed. Deal." Melvin nodded. "Bring her down. "

Dark Jerold left obediently but not happily.

FREEING HILDA

HILDA LOOKED WELL GROOMED, neat, and lovely as ever, but her face was tight and her eyes were barely open. She looked exhausted and in desperate need of sleep. Jules wanted to rush to her, hold her, and tell her everything was going to be OK. He stiffened. His fists clenched. He stayed as if he were a stone statue.

Hilda's eyes brushed over the bearded guy and the two muscle guys and then her eyes saw Charlie and they opened wide. She was about to greet him with excessive delight, but she quickly clamped her mouth tightly. This was Jules' doing. He was saving her. She had to play along with the game. An explosion of joy blossomed in her.

"These men will take you to your house." Melvin said in his calmest, sweetest tone possible. "You must treat them as your friends. They will look after you and protect you. No harm will come to you. Can you accept them?"

"Yes," Hilda said trying to sound reluctant. "I want to get home and to my own bed. I hope they keep me safe in ALL ways."

"You can guarantee that, can't you Charlie?"

"There is no way we would jeopardize our deal. She will be safe with us in every way possible." Charlie smiled knowingly at Melvin.

"Pick up your things. You are all free to go." Melvin said then added, "When do you think I'll see you again, Charlie?"

Charlie went to Jules and whispered, "When?"

Jules whispered back. "Tomorrow's the funeral, Saturday. They're closed Sunday; so it'll be Monday."

"Monday." Charlie nodded confidently.

"Good. About what time?"

Charlie went to Jules again, nodded to what Jules said and then replied, "About four Monday."

Charlie and his men picked up their belongings on the carpet and started arranging all beneath their robes. One of the men started handing the small stack in front of Jules and Jules took his recorder from his sleeve covered hand to under his arm pit again. There were no guns in Jules' small pile. Melvin and Jerold were well aware of that.

Hilda was now enjoying all that was happening. It was another of Jules' games and she loved it. Her insides were almost exploding with smiles. She was free. She was sure she'd be seeing Jules soon, but why wasn't he here, she wondered. Her energy had miraculously returned. She could breathe again.

The two muscle guys got on either side of Jules and assisted him out of the office to the elevator. Hilda wondered why such a feeble man was there. Dark Jerold followed them into the elevator. Never a word or glance was exchanged.

When the elevator stopped, Jerold stayed close to the elevator and watched as they proceeded to their car. Half way to the car, Moresee stuck his head out the window and started saying "hello" with excited barks. The closer they got the louder the barks. Hilda got to the window and petted him with delight. The delight was mutual. Moresee started licking her hand and then tried for her face.

"I've missed you too, Moresee." Hilda pulled her face away, but was delighted with Moresee's delight. How wonderful, she thought, that Moresee felt so close to her after knowing her for such a short time. He was now their dog. He was a joy and a welcome part of the family.

Jules pulled Hilda aside and opened the passenger front door for her.

"I'd rather sit in the back with Moresee, Charlie."

"Not yet, Hilda, soon. Please get in the front seat." Charlie almost whispered.

As Jules waited for Hilda to enter, he glanced back at Jerold who was writing down their license plate number. Charlie got in the driver's side and Jules sat close to Hilda. As they drove away, Jules glanced back. Jerold was gone.

"He took your license plate number." Jules said as they pulled out of the parking area.

"No problem." Charlie said casually. "I've got plenty more."

"Jules?" Hilda almost screamed.

"Yes, my dear. It's good to see you again. I haven't shaved since we parted."

"My Lord! I can't believe it! It's you! Really? Oh my! I still can't believe it! You're wonderful! I love you! You're wonderful! Thank you, my dear. I can't believe this is really you? It's such an improvement."

"Thanks a lot." Jules smiled beneath his beard.

Moresee had stuck his head between the seats and was licking Hilda's left shoulder and back.

"Does that mean I may kiss you, my dear?" Jules tested.

"Heavens no! I'm involved with Moresee right now. Maybe in a year or two."

"Oh, thank you so much. May I at least hold your hand?" He held up his left hand for approval.

Hilda touched it to make sure it was his and real. She then put both her hands around his then lifted it to her lips and kissed it three times. A question jumped into her mind and she asked,

"What is going on? Why are you dressed like this? I understand you, Charlie, and your men, but why Jules? What's the game?"

"I joined them to be invisible." Jules then explained how he had been declared mentally dangerous to her. She had been put in the Floss penthouse as protection from him. He described the hundred thousand dollar reward for his capture, and how half Charlie's money would be payment to Floss for her freedom.

"I should have turned you in up there and gotten my hundred grand now. You're costing me a lot of dough." Charlie shook his head with feigned remorse.

"Don't worry super dude." Jules replied. "You'll be well paid for what you've done for me and Moresee. You'll get your fifty grand Monday. You'll turn me in then. I'll be dressed as normal. You'll be clear and fifty grand richer I hope that will cover my living expenses."

"You can't do that!" Charlie said sharply. "You'll be tossed in the dodo can and the way they are, you might never get out."

"You did a great job up there, Charlie. I'm free as a Dodo bird and not extinct yet. You got the Floss guy to clear me. I've got it recorded. You were great up there, Charlie. I'm in the clear now. That fifty grand is just partial payment."

"Great! Then why not do it now and be finished?"

"Don't be in such a hurry. You'll ruin everything you've set up. If we did it now, your deal would be off because of deceit. You can't do it tomorrow because I have to be at J. J.'s funeral. His murderer should be there and I don't want to be recognized so I'll attend the funeral as Mohamad Moresee. Floss isn't open on Sunday; so Monday you can bring me to the Floss office. I'll be in my regular clothes. You'll be a hero and get the dough. How does that sound to you, Charlie?"

"You know I was just kidding. I never expected the fifty grand reward."

"You earned it. You're going to get it. Besides, You have no idea what I might ask you to do next."

"No problem. Fifty grand covers a lot. Where do you want me to go now?"

"Take Hilda to where my car is parked when I take my morning run. We'll let her off there and she can drive home. Is that OK with you, my dear?"

"If I can take Moresee with me, yes."

"It's a deal." Jules was delighted.

SUSPECTS

ON THE RIDE BACK to Mill Valley, Hilda had to become current with the happenings.

"Have you narrowed the suspects?" She asked.

"Only in one way." Jules replied. "Whoever is doing all this has a hell of a lot of money. Floss is big and expensive. The hundred grand reward is ridiculously high. Someone's throwing a lot of money around."

"Most the people I know with a lot of money are cheap." Hilda observed. "That's how they got a lot of money—they don't spend it."

"That's right," Jules agreed quietly. "The guys who act rich are the ones who spend other people's money—like inheritance, kids, and bums."

"And government workers." Hilda added.

"Sure, they love spending our money, but probably not for murder." Jules tilted his head. "But who knows—maybe."

"How about the Senator J. J. was running against?"

"I don't even remember his name," Jules shrugged his shoulders.

"It's Hazelton." Charlie said easily and quickly. "He uses the expensive stuff. J. J. was coming on fast. Hazelton was no longer sure of winning. He'd do everything in his power to stop J. J. Murder would be one tool."

Jules nodded. "Let's see who's at the funeral tomorrow."

"How about Dolph Briskie and that group?" Hilda was awake and happy.

"You know how cheap Dolph is. Hundred grand? I can't believe it. Anyway, Alex is covering that. He should give us the low down later today."

"If Dolph murdered J. J.," Hilda added, "look what he gained. The money and position would be his reward. Let the risk fit the crime."

"Let's see who's at the funeral." Jules repeated. "Dolph and gang could be there. We'll see tomorrow, and so could other suspects. Who we'll see tomorrow."

They were now crossing the Golden Gate Bridge. Jules eyes, as usual, floated to the top of the towers. How could he jump from there with Hilda and live?

"May I come to the funeral tomorrow, too?" Hilda's voice pleaded.

"Of course." Jules nodded beneath his heavy head of hair.

"I'm going to bring Moresee with me. I don't want to be ever alone again."

"That's fine," Jules agreed, "but don't worry. I'll be watching you closely. You'll be safe and well protected."

"Where and what time is the funeral?" Charlie asked.

"Don't know, but I'll be there a half hour early." Jules replied.

"We all will." Hilda confirmed.

They let Hilda off at Jules' car. No one was around. She and Moresee got in the car, started the engine, and drove to their home.

"The funeral is going to be interesting." Charlie mused.

"Very." Jules agreed.

Charlie and Jules drove back across the Golden Gate Bridge to their unusual residence. As usual, Jules glanced up at the towers.

ALEX RETURNS

ALEX WAS WAITING FOR them when they drove into Charlie's building.

He looked at Charlie and the guy with only forehead and eyes visible.

"Where's Jules? I've got a lot to tell him."

"Start talking, Alex, I'm anxious to hear all."

Alex shook his head twice as if trying to waken. "You've got to be kidding Come on, Jules! You look like a gorilla."

"Good! Since neither you nor Hilda recognized me, I guess I did the right thing. What did Linda tell you?" Jules asked as they headed for the open elevator.

"After we made out, she told me she wasn't married, never had been, didn't have a boyfriend, and was willing to accept me to lead her anywhere I damned pleased. Holy shit! That was not what I wanted to hear."

Alex got off the elevator with Jules. "Join me at seven for dinner." Charlie said as the elevator slowly moved up to his floors.

Jules nodded and he and Alex entered his special suite.

"OK, you and Linda had a great time. You are now a couple. That's great. Did you get any work done or did she shut your eyes"

"I had to be careful about what I said. I didn't want her to think my main interest was Dolph."

"OK, but what did you find out about Dolph and gang?"

"Not too much. Linda said Dolph hated two people—J. J. and you. He hated J. J. because J. J. was so sure and certain about everything. He hated you because you were following in his footsteps and you were getting all the favors and special attention."

"Interesting. So if he could convince the police I was a nut case, he'd have me out of the way. He'd have one score even. If he had J. J. killed or did it himself, he'd have won. His two problems would be evaporated. Plus he'd get the added benefit of being regional president."

"Linda thinks a lot of Dolph. She says he's always kind and generous to her."

"Maybe he wants what you got."

"Oh, no. He's married, you know. Linda says it's a happy marriage. He never even takes Linda to lunch. Sometimes he brings lunch to her, but that's all. She has no interest in him. You know how fat he is. He'd squash her."

"You, on the other hand, would be perfect for her."

"Forget that! There's no way I'm going to be tied to any gal. The last thing I want in the world is wife, kids, dogs, and all the problems involved. I'm free and I'm going to stay that way."

"OK, so how are we going to trap Dolph? Do you or Linda have any ideas?"

"Linda says it would be impossible for Dolph to injure or hurt anyone in even the slightest way. She really thinks highly of Dolph."

"How about his close associates, John Peter Shielding, Angela Cushing, and Roy Butler? I don't think any of them would have a problem."

"Funny, we didn't really discuss them. I only thought of Dolph."

"Dolph could have had them do it in exchange for special favors he'd give them once he was in charge."

"Favors for murder? What kind of favors would pay for murder? Maybe it makes sense to you, but not to me. I don't think SCT could afford all they would want."

"Maybe, but let's assume Dolph and his nefarious group did murder J. J. Let's say Angela let Roy and Dolph out of the car. She drove around the block so no one could see a car parked in front of J. J.'s house. Roy and Dolph enter the estate. Dolph stays hidden by the side of the house as a watchdog so no one could see him nor see Roy enter the house. Roy then goes upstairs, provokes an argument with J.

J., and throws him over the balcony onto the stone floor for J. J.'s sure death. That's the only way there would be zero witnesses. But now what?"

"It sounds like the perfect murder. It's a dead end." Alex nodded.

"Dolph will surely be at the funeral tomorrow. I bet Roy and Angela will be there, too. There has to be a way to trap them. I'll try to think of it. You try, too. We can talk it over tonight at dinner."

"I'm afraid I can't do it tonight. I already have plans."

"You do?"

"Yeah, with Linda."

"Wait a minute! You're finished with her. You got what you wanted."

"Yeah, that's right, but I've got to let her down easy. I can't hurt her."

"How about the funeral tomorrow?"

"I've got lunch with her tomorrow also. That'll probably be the end."

"Sure. Right after you're married."

"No way! I told you before—no way! We're almost finished."

"If you find a spare moment when you finish with Linda, try to think of who might have murdered J. J. Maybe Linda can clear the sex out of your mind for two or three seconds so you can think of other things. Let me know if that miracle happens."

"Don't worry about a thing, Jules. Everything is under control."

"I think you're hooked."

"I'm free and I'm going to stay free forever. I just have to be kind. I would think you of all people would understand."

"Don't worry, Alex. I understand completely. You're hooked." Jules let out a cheerful laugh and they headed to Charlies' suite for dinner.

THE FUNERAL

The Shady Oaks Cemetery was a large green field surrounded by scrub oaks. It was west of San Rafael and seven miles short of the Pacific Ocean. It had been a cattle farm. At the death of the owner, none of his children wanted to live in isolation and sold the property to the highest bidder, Shady Oaks Funeral Home.

Being a new and expensive cemetery, the center of the property was empty, green pasture, because it was still April. On the arrival of June, the hills would be tan and the dark, green oaks would enliven the hills.

The grave stones on the edges of the property were relatively new and reflected the wealth of the buried. The first grave stone rose to twenty or so feet like a triangular skyscraper. Behind it was a huge lion snarling at the world. There were many smaller sculptures of happy dogs, cats, children, and on and on. It was like going to an art show. The high ocean fog kept the day cool and relatively dismal.

The grave for J. J. had been dug, was open, and waiting. His grave stone rested at the base of the grave. It was a rectangular marble stone about five feet high by seven long. Two workers were leaning on it waiting.

It was eleven and the burial was to be at noon. Jules, Charlie, and his two hefty men had been there since ten thirty. They stood away from the grave in the shadows of some scrub oaks. There they could watch the arrivals and not be noticed. Jules in his Muslim robes waited for Hilda and Moresee to arrive.

His eyes kept searching for her. His mind was begging to see her. He'd lost her once. He could never let it happen again. But where was she? Could they have taken her back to Floss again?

The funeral procession of cars and vans arrived in a slow solemn manner. When the funeral van stopped, four men in a deliberate, pious manner carefully lifted the coffin from the van as if from an oven. The following cars started emptying.

From the car directly behind the van, a priest dressed in a black robe left with his Bible in hand. Behind him J. J.'s brother, Paul, jumped out, as if going to a party. His attire was a black sport jacket, bright blue sport shirt, and flaming yellow pants. With Paul was Oliver, dressed completely in black, with white shirt and a black bow tie. They walked behind the solemn priest and ahead of the four carrying the casket.

From the next car emerged Dolph Briskie, Angela Cushing, John Peter Shielding, and Roy Butler. Dolph was dressed in appropriate black jacket and dark grey pants. His width served as a shield to the others who wore their usual business clothes. The funeral was a brief inconvenience. The car behind Dolph unloaded three guys.

Charlie pointed to the tall lanky one. "That's Senator Hazelton. He looks like he needs something to cheer him up. I'll see him later."

There were two other cars. Jules recognized J. J.'s cook and housecleaner. The last vehicle was a van clearly marked "Park Ranger." The driver jumped out of the van and opened the back door. Two Rangers sauntered out.

To Jules the motive for murder was clear except for Senator Hazelton. It was for J. J.'s money—clear and simple. The Senator was eliminated because he didn't need the money. He had become a millionaire by being a public servant.

Jules figured he wouldn't murder to win an election. He had had twelve years as a public servant. He'd made his fortune. He could retire and afford his drugs.

J. J.'s brother, Paul, and J. J.'s butler, Oliver, were now rich. Paul could spend wildly and recklessly and still have millions left. He'd never have to work or worry or ask his brother for money. Oliver could return home to England as a millionaire. They both had good motives for murder and they could have worked together and that is why there were no witnesses for the murder.

Dolph and crew had two good motives—money and power. As Dolph walked toward the gravesite, he puffed his chest out so far that it almost reached his stomach. He was trying to look serious and important, but the joy radiating from his eyes and the corners of his mouth dominated. Angela's lips were tucked in tightly as if expecting problems. John Peter Shielding looked upset at having to attend. Roy Butler looked bored. Jules eliminated John Peter Shielding. He was a number, not a human. The other three had good motives.

His eyes drifted over the others. The household staff had no reason for murder. They now had to look for new jobs that probably would not be nearly as good. The Park Rangers were just doing their job. None of the groups that J. J. had offended were present.

All gathered in front of the priest, the coffin, and the gravesite. The Rangers stood about ten yards behind.

Jules heard a car screech to a stop. Everyone looked. even the priest who was about to begin the ceremony. It was Hilda and More-see. She opened her door and slammed it. She then opened the door for Moresee and slammed again.

She then looked at all the eyes watching her and her shoulders sank with embarrassment. She put Moresee on a leash and tried to walk quickly and invisibly toward the pious ceremony.

Moresee would have none of it. He was delighted to be in the open to visit new worlds. Hilda had to wrap the leash around her right hand so it was locked tightly. Moresee was oblivious to the leash and seemed to enjoy pulling Hilda up the hill. His stub of a tail was wagging as much as it could. He smelled Jules and was going to rush to say "Hello."

Moresee stopped suddenly. His head snapped around and he let out a vicious snarl and started pulling Hilda toward the two Park Rangers and their driver.

"No, Moresee! NO!" Hilda almost screamed as she was struggling to keep upright. She couldn't loosen the leash to free her hand. Jules ran to help when Moresee stopped directly in front of one of the Rangers.

Moresee crouched with teeth bared and a ferocious growl. He wanted to attack the Ranger.

Jules lifted the fifty-pound Moresee into his robe-covered arms.

"What the hell is that dog doing here?" The Ranger had taken two steps backward and both his arms were outstretched for protection. "What the hell are you doing with a dog at a funeral? Put him in the back of our van."

"No!" Hilda said sharply. "What are you doing here? This is not public grounds. This is privately owned. You don't belong here. Why are you here? Why of all the people in the world does my dog hate you? I now know exactly why. He was the sole witness of YOU murdering his master, J. J. You are here at J. J.'s funeral

because you murdered him and want to see him buried and your terrible deed buried with him. That's why you are here. You are a murderer! You murdered J. J. And I'm going to prove it and put YOU in prison on murderer's row! That's where you belong and that's where you're going to be. I promise you!"

"You, lady, are as crazy as your husband. You need help. Both of you get in my van." The Ranger said authoritatively. He nodded to bearded Jules who was still carrying Moresee. "Bring them!"

"Your name please, kind sir." Jules tried hard to sound foreign.

"Edwards, John Edwards."

"And yours, kind sir?" Jules asked Edward's boss.

"Tom Fitzgerald. What the hell do you need our names for?"

"I always need to know who to thank in order to send appropriate rewards." Jules replied with a short bow. "And you, sir?" He asked the driver.

"Pete Jonas." The driver mumbled as if annoyed.

"Thank you Mr. Edwards. Thank you Mr. Fitzgerald. Thank you Mr. Jonas. Thank you for allowing me to help you. I'll put this woman and her vicious dog in the back of your van. Thank you, thank you." Jules backed away as well as he could carrying Moresee and slightly bowing to each one. He took Hilda by the hand and he kept bowing and backing until the steep hill made him turn.

Jules led Hilda to the Ranger's van. Hilda was still furious but felt protected by her Muslim husband. Jules led her around to the back of the van where they were out of sight. He opened the back door, put Moresee down, gave Hilda the leash.

"Open the door, wait, then slam it shut." Jules whispered.

As Hilda followed instructions, Jules reached under his robe, pulled a pocket knife from his pocket, opened one of the blades, and with a hard blow punched a hole in the rear tire. He timed it carefully with the door slam. He then extracted the knife, put it back in his pocket, and led Hilda to their car as he listened to the musical hiss of the escaping air. Jules opened the doors to their car and in they got.

"What the hell's going on?" Fitzgerald heard the door slam as Moresee was put in Jules' car and another as Hilda got in and the final one when Jules got in, turned on the engine and backed to an area to turn around and leave.

"That's the wrong car! The van! My van!" Edwards shouted to Jules. "What the hell's the matter with him?"

"He's new to the country." Charlie said quickly. "He probably thought you wanted him to take her home. He doesn't understand too good yet."

The priest was watching the incident with open Bible and open mouth. Dolph was shaking his head as if trying to waken. His belly had regained its rightful place of soaring over his chest. Angela had her hands on her hips as if angry with the interruption. John Peter Shielding looked bored. He might play games on his cell phone. Roy Butler was ready for a fight, and hoped for it to happen. The Senator kept looking at Charlie longing for some happiness. The others just watched in shocked disbelief.

"Son-of-a-bitch! Come on," the accused Ranger shouted to his partner. "We've got to stop them!" They started running toward their van.

As their doors of their van closed and the engine started, there was a moment of silence. The Priest cleared his voice, "Dear relatives and friends of the late, wonderful, generous, and unforgettable, Jerry Jackson—"

The engine stopped. The van's doors opened and slammed shut again as Ranger John Edwards rushed to look as his rear tire.

The shouted filthy words he used had never been heard before at a funeral.

THE RIDE HOME

JULES GOT TO THE MAIN road but travelled just a few hundred yards, saw a small, unused dirt road, and took it. It was as he hoped—the other side of the cemetery. The scrub oaks were plentiful, tight, and close to the ground. They easily and completely concealed their car. He reached in his pocket and dialed.

"We're on the other side of the cemetery, Charlie. Any extra plates?"

"Hell yes. Don't go anywhere naked."

"As soon as they leave, drive over here. I need two new plates."

"Hell, they left just a few minutes after you. They changed that tire race car fast. I'll be right over."

He put the phone on the dashboard, got out of the car, and disrobed his Muslim attire. With the overhead fog and the cool ocean breeze, the outfit had been comfortably warm. Now with it off, he became aware of brisk air. He hurried to the back of the car, threw open the door, and pulled Moresee to him.

"You, my boy, are the best! You solved what none of us humans could. You are good. No, you are wonderful. No, you are sensational. You are super dog. J. J. has to be happy sleeping in his grave. You made him so. You took care of your master. Good boy, Moresee." With this Jules rubbed Moresee's nose, head, back, and chest vigorously. Moresee was delighted and content.

"Then you're not angry with us?" Hilda looked worried.

"Just the opposite. That part of the case is closed. We know who murdered J. J. But what the hell was the reason? Why would a park ranger go to an important guy's house and get angry enough to throw him over the railing to kill him? It doesn't make sense."

At that moment Charlie and his henchmen drove in. As Charlie got out of the car, Jules handed him his Muslim attire and Charlie handed him the plates.

"You know what's happening Monday, don't you?" Charlie asked.

Jules looked at him and squinted. There were so many things happening that Jules couldn't think of one particular thing. He looked hard at Charlie. Was this a game? Jules shook his head.

"With you standing beside me, I get fifty tax free grand, partner old buddy."

"That's right." Jules nodded.

"What's that for?" Hilda asked.

"I stayed at his hotel." Jules replied with a smile. "That's the cost per night. It's quite a hotel."

"It must be." Hilda was not smiling.

Jules explained the situation and when finished added, "That's why I have to stay at his lavish hotel again tonight. He's bringing me in tomorrow, and going home with fifty grand. Pretty good deal for him. You're free and I'll be free, too."

"I hope so but you may be back in jail." Hilda was not pleased.

"No way," Jules smiled. "I have it all recorded. They can test the recording all they want but they'll never find fault with it. It has not been tampered in any way. Much to their frustration, they'll have to let me go. I'll be free again and can wear my regular clothes and can live in our house with my dear, wonderful wife."

"I still don't like it. Maybe you didn't alter the recording, but that doesn't mean they can't and won't. They want you out of their way and in jail. Can't you see that?"

"Don't get worried. I'm safe."

"Of course I'm worried. I know what they've done to me and now I know what they've done to you. They made you out officially to be a mental case. What if one little thing goes wrong with your recording? You'll be back in jail and we'll both be ruined. Please don't forget our new baby."

"OK," Jules agreed, "What do you want me to do?"

Hilda turned to Charlie. "Can you copy his recording?"

"I copied it at the time."

"Did your men, too?"

"No."

"They both must have phones," Hilda continued. "Could you have both phones copy the conversation and loan one of the phones to me? I'll only keep it until Jules is completely cleared."

Charlie nodded, gave his phone to one of the men, had the conversation copied on both phones, and handed one to Hilda. She took it as if she were being handed a valuable jewel and carefully tucked it into her purse.

"Thank you, Charlie. Thanks a lot."

Charlie smiled and nodded. He turned to Jules. "Now what? You going to ride back with me?"

"No, I'll drive Hilda to your fancy hotel so she knows where it is and then she can drive home. First, I'm going to visit J. J. and say good-bye. Second is for you. As you know, I have all their names—J. J.'s murderer who Moresee attacked, his boss, and the driver. Just a minute—I'll write them all down for you."

Jules printed the names as best as he could spell them, handed them to Charlie, and watched as Charlie and his bodyguards left.

As Charlie and his men drove away. Jules and Hilda watched in silence. Jules opened the car door for her and they drove back to J. J.'s grave. The two workmen needed a few more shovels of dirt to complete their job. Jules and Hilda stayed in their car, watched and waited, and when the men were finished and left, Jules opened Hilda's door and they walked to the gravesite.

Jules bowed his head in reverence, closed his eyes, and stayed silent as a salute to J. J. Then he spoke softly so only Hilda and Moresee could hear.

"I miss you, J. J. You were the father I had always wanted. You steered and shaped my life. You changed me from a destroyer to a builder. Instead of hiding what I am, like Charlie has to do, I can proudly puff out my chest and tell what I do to help build our country. You gave me a growing and generous salary. You gave me a terrific house. You taught me how to be a trusted husband which cements our marriage and will make a good home for our baby. Thank you, J. J. I miss you.

"But I'm not finished. I now know your murderer. He will be brought to justice. I will not rest until that is done. I don't care the cost. It will be done so that you can rest in peace with God, dear J. J. Amen."

Jules closed his eyes and stood over the grave as if sending his words to the heavens. He took a deep breath, opened his eyes, tried to smile at Hilda, took her hand and they walked silently to the car. The wind was pushing the cold fog as if angry.

After a long bout of silence, Jules shook his head and asked, "Why the hell would a park ranger murder J. J.? It doesn't make sense."

Hilda waited quietly before replying. "I think you told me quite a while ago, my dear, that a park ranger gave J. J. a ticket because of what Moresee did on one of his walks on the trail."

"Yeah, sure. He was given a ticket for not picking up Moresee's poop in the fields." Jules shook his head and even had a short laugh. "That's not a reason for murder. Besides, that was a quite a while ago."

"Yes, it was before J. J. became prominent in the race for Senator. That could have changed everything."

Jules shook his head. "I don't get it."

"John Edwards and all the public employees were safe when J. J. was just like us—nothing. When J. J. started gaining rapidly in the polls where it would be possible for him to be elected Senator, J. J. became a worry. If elected, J. J. would no longer be below them he would be above them. He could destroy them."

"Like how?"

"Lose their jobs, retirement, and all the other fantastic benefits they receive at our expense. What if they went over to J. J. to discuss it? What if J. J. laughed at them? What if in a momentary fit of rage they threw J. J. over the rail to his death and their safety?"

"Because of dog poop?"

"No, because they have fantastic benefits which we pay for. We pay—they collect. Look at all they could lose—huge salaries for little work, massive vacation time and sick leave, they never miss a holiday, and they can retire early and collect more money than when they worked. They will do anything to protect all this. If J. J. had been elected, they could have lost everything. He was a threat. They are government workers paid to serve us. They don't."

Jules nodded. After a short while he said, "You and Moresee are solving everything. I haven't solved a damn thing. I just keep getting in trouble. Thank you. Thank you. But now I have a major problem and I hope you can solve this also—how the hell can I accuse a park ranger of murder let alone convict him? What can I do? Maybe I should teach Moresee to talk so he could testify against him. Other than that, it's hopeless. He is the government. He has the power. I have none. How the hell can we do a damn thing?"

"You'll think of a way." Hilda replied with quiet confidence.

They rode in silence the rest of the trip to Charlie's building. When Jules drove down the alley to Charlie's apartment building, Hilda looked at each decrepit building and gasped.

"This is the slums. How could anyone possible live here—especially Charlie?"

"You're right. The outside is bad, the inside is worse, but when you open a door and enter the suites, you'll think you're in a palace. Would you like to see?"

"Not now. I want to get back to our own home and bed. Hurry. Our home is an empty house without you. You are needed. I miss you."

"I'll get it done as fast as I can. On our trip I got an idea."

"Good!"

"I hope it works."

"It will. Hurry home!"

"Wait here for a minute. We have to change the plates back." Jules waived to one of Charlie's men, handed him the correct license plates, kissed Hilda through the open driver's window, and entered Charlie's building.

Jules stayed where with Charlie through the weekend. Charlie had to run his men and business. Jules was anxious for Monday to come. He spent little time with Charlie, made some calls to Hilda on the throw-aways, and did a lot of walking to try to make up for the running he was missing. He was delighted when Monday arrived.

EASY MONEY?

As he entered Charlie's suite, Charlie rose from his leather chair and bowed. "I never thought you were worth a penny. Now you're a beautiful hunk of dough. Fifty grand! J. J. would be proud."

Jules smiled and shook his head, "Isn't it wild that I've become the bad guy for wanting to solve a murder? I'm the villain. Now that I know the murderer I'll probably be the next one they'll want to kill."

"Don't worry. Put on your robes. Join us again. You'll be safe."

Jules shook his head in despair. "Isn't that amazing? Yes, that way I'd be on equal footing with our public servants—maybe even above them. Yeah, Charlie, maybe that's what I have to do."

"Then you'd better become a Muslim. If you go parading around in their robes as a disguise, you'll have new enemies. Don't do it."

Jules said nothing but shook his head in agreement.

"I have to make a couple of calls before we go." Charlie said.

"Sure, but one more thing. I know all the names of the murderer and gang, but I need their addresses, too."

"Oh shit! Will it never end? OK. OK, I'll do my best."

"Those three are always together even at work. Find their work van and when the day is done, get their license plate numbers, and get the rest from there. It should be easy for your guys."

"Now you're telling me how to run my business? Maybe you should join back up with us."

"The way all this is going you never know. It might be my only option. I just hope that recording of Floss will clear me."

"No problem. Mr. Floss's voice will clear you. No problem. If they ruin yours—we have three more. Don't worry. I'll get fifty grand and you'll be cleared. They will think your brain is normal and I'll try not to correct them."

"Thanks, I guess."

"I've got to call good old Floss and get everything prepared." With this Charlie looked at Floss' business card, took a throw-away phone from his pocket and dialed.

"Good-morning. Please tell Mr. Floss I have Jules Cameron in my custody."

There was a lengthy pause.

"Yes, Mr. Floss, I have Jules Cameron right here with me. Here's the deal. I need to be paid when I hand him over to you. I want fifty grand in unmarked hundred dollar bills. You tell me when I can bring him in."

There was another lengthy pause.

"OK! You say you have that amount of cash right now. That's perfect. We'll be there shortly. I'll keep Cameron in the car in case there's some problem. If everything is clean, we'll close the deal."

After hanging up, he turned to Jules and smiled. "They're trying to trace the call." With this he totally destroyed the phone.

"We're going to take two cars." Charlie continued. "I'll drive one car alone. You will be tied up neatly and ride with my two men in another car. You will follow me. I'll park and then join you in your car. Got it?"

"What's the deal?" Jules asked.

"I'm sure they won't follow us. The car we park in their garage they'll mark in an almost impossible way for anyone else to find. When we leave, they'll quickly find that car. Me and my guys will get in the other car and drive away. They'll find the marked car right where we parked it. They can have it. We'll get another one. No problem."

Jules nodded. This was getting interesting.

Charlie nodded to his men and they got some long rope and tied Jules' legs, his hands behind his back, and then they roped three times around his chest and arms and tied all but the leg ropes tightly.

"Does it have to be this tight? I'm not going to run away."

"It has to be professional and secure."

"What's your schedule with me?"

"I'll leave you at Floss. If there's any problem, I'll leave the extra tapes with Hilda. You've got your tape plus the extras. That should clear you."

"So it's good-bye for a while."

"They can't know that we are connected in any way."

"Got it. As soon as Hilda recovers, it'll be dinner time again."

"It's a deal. OK guys, get him in the Plymouth van. I'm taking the Audi. Follow me."

With a powerful guy on each side, they dragged Jules to the Plymouth. It obviously had not been used for a while as its black paint was muted with dust.

The men carefully donned rubber gloves, lifted Jules into the back seat, and they drove off. The motor sounded good and the ride was smooth.

They followed Charlie on Bryant, turned right on 6th Street, up to Folsom, right again, and drove to a large seemingly deserted building in an isolated area. Parking was readily available. Charlie parked and got in the back seat with Jules.

As they drove into the parking area beneath the Floss Building, Charlie turned to Jules. "When you get up there, try not to say one word. They recorded when you were a Muslim and if you say anything they'll find out you were that Muslim. That could be a problem. Let them call the police. You'll go to jail. Then you can talk and give them your recording. Any problem, call Hilda. She'll have the other recordings."

Jules nodded. He was fully aware of the situation.

With the car parked, Charlie walked to the elevator in the parking area. Jules watched as the elevator door closed and Charlie rose for his appointment. About fifteen minutes later Charlie reappeared with two other men.

"Get him out and bring him up." Charlie spoke sharply to his men and they followed his instructions.

They pulled Jules out as if he were a bag of dirty clothes. He landed first on his knees, then was turned around to his fanny, his back, and then lifted sharply to his feet. Jules remained silent.

"Walk in front and carefully. Is of your guys armed?" One of the Floss guards asked.

"No." Charlie confirmed.

"Don't anyone put their hand in their robe for any reason." The other guard warned with a deadly serious voice.

"Understood." Charlie acknowledged.

"And do your men understand what I said?"

"Yeah." Charlie replied, "Perfectly. No problem now or ever."

Charlie's two men each put an arm behind Jules' back and dragged him into the elevator, out again and then down the hallway to Mr. Floss's office door. A Floss man knocked once, opened the door, and entered. Floss was seated behind his desk and looked ready to duck beneath it to escape potential bullets. He watched each one with nervous eyes.

"Did you frisk them?" Floss asked.

"No. They know they can't put their hands in their robes for any reason."

"I guess that will do. What do you have to say for yourself?" He asked Jules.

Jules gave a negative shake to his head.

"The cat got your tongue?"

Jules stared at him and remained silent.

"I guess I can understand that." Floss grinned and almost smiled. His eyes kept watching the others for any possible problem.

"He's all yours." Charlie spoke sharply. "Where my dough?"

Floss lifted a bag beneath his desk, put it on the top of the desk, but stayed seated behind the desk's protection.

"Do you want to count it?" Floss suggested.

"You'd better do the right thing." Charlie replied. "If it's wrong, you'll get some powerful people real angry. For you own health, you don't want that."

"How do I know this is Jules Cameron?"

"You don't cheat me, I don't cheat you. Simple as that." Charlie took the bag, nodded to Floss, and he and his two men backed to the door and left.

Floss got on his phone and called the police. It took about fifteen minutes for them to arrive. Along with them was the psychologist who glared at Jules.

"You have severe problems and you've made the problems even more severe. I trusted you. You tried to ruin me. Now you will be ruined. Take off those ropes." He instructed the two policemen. "Put cuffs on his hands and ankles."

When that was done, Mr. Floss asked, "When should I expect the reward check?"

The two policemen looked at each other hoping for the answer. The doctor answered, "It'll be a government check. You'll probably get it in a week or two."

Floss shook his head with disgust but accepted the information.

The two policeman guided Jules out the door, to the elevator and down to their patrol car. Ankle and wrist cuffed Jules was lifted into the backseat of the car and the doctor sat beside him.

"With all my studies, I felt confident I could trust you. Why did you turn on me and become an escaped criminal?"

"I did it to save my wife. When we get to the station, I'll play the information and all will become clear to you."

The doctor shook his head. "There is no reasonable explanation for what you did. You made a huge mental mistake and you'll pay for it mightily."

Jules stayed quiet the rest of the way to the police station.

PROBLEMS MAGNIFY

THE PSYCHOLOGIST WALKED TIGHTLY close to Jules as if they were tied together. The doctor's fury was quite obvious. When they got to an interrogation room, only the doctor entered with him.

"I need the police chief and several other people to be here," Jules said enthusiastically.

The doctor nodded his head to the window, turned back to Jules and said, "This better be damn important or this will be your new home."

Jules said nothing. They waited in silence for the Chief of Police and three other men to arrive.

"What's going on?" The Chief asked.

"In my left front pocket there's a tape. Please take it out and play it for all to hear. Mr. Floss of the Floss Detective Agency is doing the talking."

The chief nodded and one of the men reached into Jules' pocket, pulled out the tape, and turned it on. When the tape ended, all were silent and looked straight ahead.

Jules let the silence stay. At what he thought was the correct moment he said, "According to Mr. Floss I was set-up. I have no mental problems. He knew it and said so. He was paid to keep me from discovering who murdered Jerry Jackson. My wife was taken prisoner by the Floss Agency supposedly to protect her from me. The last thing I would ever do would be to harm my dear wife in any way. They took her without my knowledge of where she was or who had taken her with the implied threat evil people had kidnapped her and she would be killed if I continued to look for J. J.'s murderer or murderers. They expected me to turn all my attention to looking for her. I did. I found her. She is now safe in our home. Please take off these shackles so I can join her."

The stunned silence continued. Finally, the Police Chief nodded. "Remove the cuffs. You're free to go." As the cuffs were removed, the Chief continued. "How did this nonsense get started? You, you," he pointed at each officer, "find out who started this. This is disgraceful and we will get the blame for something we didn't do. Find out!"

The two police officers almost ran from the room.

Jules then told of how everything had happened when he went to take his morning run and he had called the police station because he was worried about who was following him at this early time of the morning. He then explained that the two following him were detectives from the Floss Agency and they claimed he was dangerous and had mental problems the proof was that he wouldn't accept the fact the police had said the case was closed and J. J.'s death was an accident.

"And why do you think it wasn't?" the Chief asked.

"J. J. was a small man. The bannister was chest high. It was almost impossible for him to fall over it. He had to be lifted and thrown to his death. I just want to find out who did that."

The Chief picked up the phone. "Have Detective Smith come here immediately."

"Wouldn't be wisest if I gave him one more mental exam?" The psychologist asked.

"We are the ones who've been tricked. This game is over. He is free to go. Do you have transportation?" He asked Jules.

"No, sir."

"You want to talk to him? Take him to his house." He nodded to the psychologist.

"Thank you, sir," Jules said as the left, "I'm sorry for the doubts I had about the police. Those doubts are gone one hundred percent."

As Jules and the psychologist left, Detective Smith entered.

NEW DEVELOPMENTS

JULES GOT IN THE front seat of a light brown, shiny, new Tesla. He opened the door with extreme caution. He didn't want to break, mar, or even leave a fingerprint. He didn't want to rouse any more fury in the doctor.

As he carefully seated himself, the doctor got behind the wheel, slammed his door, and started the engine. As they silently started to move, Jules spoke,

"Excuse me, Doctor, but I've forgotten your name."

"Dr. Stoulk. That seems to be the only thing you've forgotten." His tone was sharp and terse.

"I'm sorry you're angry."

"I did you a favor and how do you repay me? With humiliation."

"I would think you'd be pleased to know I'm sane and problem free."

"That's the last thing in the world you are. You are a factory of problems."

"Like what?"

"I don't have time to go into all of them. I'll just ask one question and your answer will display you. Do you think there is such a thing as God?"

"Of course. I know God exists."

"There you are." The doctor replied with a smug smile.

"So knowing there is a God is a mental problem?"

"The worst kind. You justify your and others actions based on a book that's thousands of years old and without any scientific foundation."

"I've never read the Bible. I don't know what it says."

"That's even worse. You base your life on nothing. You're dangerous. You definitely need help."

"Well, I want to learn, Doctor. What is your proof that God does not exist?"

"Nothing stays static. Things change. Everything evolves."

"And how long does it take for evolution to take place."

"It is happening every moment. Everything is changing."

"I don't see where anything is different. Everything seems the same to me."

"Of course it does. You can't see evolution. It takes hundreds of years. It is gradual."

"Well, Doctor, it's been two thousand years since the days of Jesus. What animal has changed? It seems to me that lions are still lions, sheep are sheep, dogs are dogs and all the animals, trees, grasses look the same as they were two thousand years ago. What new animals, trees or whatever do we have? And if evolution were real and after millions of years of everything evolving, wouldn't new things be popping up all around us? They're not. It seems to me our main problem is extinction. We're working like crazy to save certain plants and animals from extinction. Doesn't the fear of extinction and no new species dent the theory of evolution?"

"You are sick—very sick. You'll be in some doctor's care sooner than you can imagine, Here's your house. Good riddance and goodbye but not for long."

Jules closed the door softly. Dr. Stoulk squealed the tires in his fury to leave. Jules watched for a moment, turned, and there was Hilda and Moresee. Behind them two workmen were placing bars across their front door.

"What's going on?"

"Our house has been condemned. We can't go in." Hilda replied. Her eyes were moist. "Here's a letter to you from one of Charlie's men."

He took the envelope but ignored it. "This has to be a mistake. Who have you called?"

"The County of Marin. I've tried to get answers, but they keep switching me to this line then another and another endlessly. I can never get to talk to anyone. Also, our bank account is frozen. I can't get any money. This is awful, dear. I don't know what to do." She covered her eyes briefly in fear of tears.

"Let me have your phone. Mine is still at the Police Station as evidence of what Floss did to us."

Hilda quickly hand her phone and Jules dialed.

"This is Jules Cameron. I talked to the Police Chief earlier this morning. It is important I talk to him again."

There was a brief pause. The Police Chief answered and Jules explained the situation. After hanging up he smiled and said to Hilda,

"The Chief will check it out immediately. He won't be treated like dirt. He'll get some answers."

"How soon?"

"I don't know."

"Where are we going to sleep tonight?"

"I'll call Charlie."

"No, no. I do not want to sleep in the slums."

"As I told you, yes, the outside is a mess, but the rooms are great."

"I will not sleep in that building. I don't care how lovely or beautiful the rooms are. It's the dangerous part of San Francisco. I have your baby. I don't want you, me, or our baby to have any association with filth and evil."

"It's not really that bad."

"It is to me. Charlie's apartment is out."

"I guess we're going to sleep on our lawn. I'll go in and get some sleeping bags."

"You can't go in. No one can."

"I can't go into my own house?"

"It's condemned, dear. No one can go in."

"This is crazy. What the hell can we do?"

"While you were at the police station, I desperately tried to think of any and all possibilities. I came up with one—Paul."

"Paul? Who's Paul?"

"J. J.'s brother. We met him and had a conversation with him right after J. J.'s death. If he's moved to the big house, his house would be available. If he's still in his house, J. J.'s house would be available."

"Do you think we could move in? What a thought. What do you suggest?"

"I think we should drive over there right now and ask him. If the answer is 'no' we'll have to think of something else. It's worth the try. But what are we going to do about money? We can't ask him for room, board, and money."

"I'll call Charlie. I can get a hunk of cash from him. I have enough cash in pocket to get us by for a day or two. Let's go see Paul." Jules opened the car door for Hilda. Moresee followed and sat between her legs. Jules rushed around to his door. Before he started the engine, he opened the envelope from Charlie and read, "Ranger John Edwards, his boss Tom Fitzgerald, driver Pete Jonas." Their phone numbers and addresses were below each name. Perfect, Jules thought.

Jules thought of all of Paul's possible replies. How could he convince Paul to let them stay? Paul had been obvious in his dislike for him. With strategies still racing, they arrived at J. J.'s mansion. Hilda waited for Jules to open her door. Moresee was kept in the car. They walked to the mansion's front door. They rang the bell. They knocked. They waited. No answer. They then headed down to Paul's house.

Jules knocked firmly once. No noise. They waited and finally heard steps hurrying down a staircase. The door opened and Paul stepped back with surprise.

"You!" Paul shook his head. "Well at least you're not a lawyer. Now who the hell do you think I murdered?"

"You are innocent." Jules smiled. "We do not suspect you of anything. We came here to ask your help. We are now homeless. The wonderful house J. J. provided for us has been condemned by the county. We have no place to stay and thought you might be able to help."

"How the hell do you expect me to help? I'm not in the real estate business. Hell, I'm not in any business except paying the damn lawyers all damn day and night. They're killing me. My life is being ruined. God, I wish J. J. were still alive. Now why are you here?"

"We know who murdered J. J.," Jules replied.

"Great! Who? Tell me and I'll murder him."

"May we come in to discuss this?" Hilda asked with a soft smile.

"You, lovely lady, may come in any damn time you please. You're Hilda, right?"

"Right. May we both come in?"

"And what's his name?" He asked Hilda.

"He is the famous detective, Jules Cameron. He can help you solve the problems you're having with attorneys."

"Come on in! You are both welcome. Yes, even you, Famous Detective, Jules," He led him to the pool table, pulled two folded canvas beach chairs, unfolded them, motioned for them to sit down, and he sat on the edge of the pool table.

"Now, Famous Detective, who killed my brother?"

"We have to put things in order, Mr. Jackson. I realize what is important to you, but what is important to me and my wife is that the county has impounded our home. They have frozen our bank account so we have no money. My wife is pregnant, and we need help."

"So what the hell do you want? You want me to give you money? What the hell is this?"

"We need a place to stay." Hilda said softly. "Since only Oliver is staying in J. J.'s house, we thought we might be able to stay there, too. I'm sure if J. J. were alive he'd insist on it. May we stay in J. J.'s house until this mess is settled?"

"Oliver will be leaving as soon as he gets his money from the will." Paul shook his head, rubbed his hair, and finally said, "Yeah, OK. What a damn mess! Now tell me who murdered J. J.?"

"May I please have a piece of paper and a pencil so I can make a copy for myself?"

"Shit! For a Famous Detective you don't have a damn thing." He got what Jules requested and Jules handed Paul the information Charlie had given him. Paul looked at the three names, addresses, and phone numbers. "Who the hell are they?"

Jules quietly and patiently explained the entire situation including Moresee wanting to attack Ranger John Edwards at the funeral. He finished by saying, "Since Moresee can't talk, there's no way to bring Edwards to justice."

"So who are these other two guys?"

"Jonas is the driver and Fitzgerald is his boss."

"Were they all involved?"

"I assume so because they're always together now as if stuck on fly paper."

"Jonas was probably driving around the block while the two went in to talk to J. J. They probably spilled their guts when they got back into the car and Jonas heard everything. Interesting. Now I've got another deal for you. I'm being pestered by the guys who set J. J. up for election to take his spot. Shit no! That's talk, talk, talk—never ending talk. Not interested. Since you're going to be staying here and you've been brainwashed by J. J., you take it. How about it?"

"You've got to be kidding." Jules laughed.

"Yes, he will." Hilda said quickly and sharply.

"Come on, my dear. I'm not a politician. I don't even know what to say."

"If you run as Senator, you will not be on equal status with the public employees. You will be above them. They will have to listen to you, pay attention, and fear you. You have to do it. It's your best way to solve J. J.'s murder."

Jules looked from Hilda to Paul and back and forth myriad times. He kept turning it over in his mind and finally said, "OK. I'll do it. When must I give my acceptance speech?"

"In two nights right here. I'll call the Oliver and he'll set you up. They'll be happy and off my back. I'll be happy. Everyone will be happy."

"Except me." Jules' head dropped. "Oliver can do all this?"

"Of course. You think I could do it? No way! That's work. I want nothing to do with that. He set it all up for J. J. He knows everyone involved. I'll call him when you leave. He'll get it all arranged. It'll be easy. Prepare a good speech."

"No problem. I'll start the speech by asking, who can loan me a dime?"

"You need money? How much do you need? You can have whatever you need. I've never seen so much money. Oh, and by the way, as payment you're now designated to talk to all the lawyers that pester me. Is that a deal?"

"Hilda, for God's sake save me. Can you handle the lawyers?"

"Of course, my dear." Hilda nodded. "I'll talk to them."

"It's all working out just fine." Paul smiled and took a deep breath. "Maybe my life will get back to somewhat normal. How about you and me having some private meetings?" He asked Hilda.

"Please try to remember that I'm pregnant with my first child."

"OK, it's back to no work for me. That's what I love. Here are the keys to J. J.'s house. I'll call Oliver and tell him the new deal. Do you need him?"

"Not at all." Hilda replied. "I'm surprised he's still here."

"He's waiting for the reading of the will. When he gets his share, he's gone. Do you have clothes and things?"

"No," Hilda replied, "our house is sealed. What we have on and in the car is all we have."

"J. J. never threw away anything. I'm sure there's some of Lydia's clothes there. Use them. They're yours. Now you," he nodded to Jules, "are a different problem. J. J. was a hell of a lot shorter than you. I guess you're stuck with the clothes you're got. You're going to be a smelly mess."

"If I had some money, I'd buy some new clothes."

"How quickly I forgot. How much?"

"Two grand should solve my problems."

"My check book is in my pocket because I'm writing checks to someone every five minutes." Paul pulled out his check book, "What's your last name?"

"Cameron."

The check was written and handed to Jules. Jules thanked him, Hilda smiled and they headed for their new home.

NEW EVERYTHING

As THEY WALKED TOWARD their car, Jules stumbled a couple of times. Hilda said nothing but gripped his arm tighter.

"Moresee is going to be happy to be back in his old home." She said as they reached the car.

"What a mess!" Jules kept shaking his head. "How did this happen to me? I can't believe it. Now one thing for you—please never introduce me again as a 'famous or otherwise detective'. I haven't solved a damn thing—nothing. Yes, things keep falling in my lap to make me look good, but not by what I've done. It's what you've done or Moresee or happenstance but never me. So please don't embarrass me again. I'm not a detective let alone a famous one."

"Yes, my dear." Hilda had a slight smile on her face. "Our house is temporarily unavailable, but our replacement isn't so bad, is it?"

"It's fantastic, and again, it was a great suggestion, my dear."

"What are your plans now?"

"My head's still spinning. I've got to get it all straightened out."

"We don't have to worry about our current residence. We are safely and securely located. We don't have to worry about money. Paul will take care of that as long as we keep him from doing any work. I'll make sure of that."

"I could always get some cash from Charley."

"Never! Please don't consider that for a moment. That's tainted money. We do not want to be tainted in any way. Forget Charley. anyway"

"He has contacts that can help us."

"Fine. Use his contacts but not his money."

Jules took his key and opened the front door of J. J.'s house. As they entered, Oliver was coming down the circular staircase.

"Forgive me, dear ones, for not getting the door for you." Oliver almost started to run.

"No problem," Jules raised his hand to slow him. "Take your time."

As Oliver hurried to them, Hilda spoke first, "I have Moresee in the car. I'll bring him in."

"How wonderful!" Oliver raised his hands. "He'll be right at home. He's a marvelous dog—almost a person." When Hilda left, Oliver continued. "Mr. Paul said you'd take J. J.'s spot in the election."

Jules nodded but uncertainty flooded his mind.

"That's nice." Oliver looked relieved. "Mr. Paul would have made a mess of everything. He was asking me what he should say. I couldn't tell him. I have no idea what American people want to hear. It would have been an embarrassing mess. It is wonderful you have come along. You have two nights and a whole day to work it out in your mind. I was afraid Mr. Paul would disgrace Mr. Jackson."

"I'm not sure people will find what I say interesting. Are you going to notify the newspapers also?" Jules asked.

"Only if you say so, sir."

"I say so. Also, make sure you tell them about our house being impounded."

"That's not a positive, sir. It's quite hurtful."

"They'll check it out and maybe find out the reason."

"Your disgrace will cover the front pages, sir. Nothing good will be said of you."

"I understand. Now I'm an unknown. That will make me well known."

"Yes, sir, but maybe not in the best possible way, sir."

"You're absolutely right, Oliver, but I insist. My name must ring a bell."

"It will be done, sir." Oliver closed his eyes in despair.

Hilda walked in with unleashed Moresee who saw Oliver rushed to him, jumped onto his right leg with tail wagging, and rubbed his nose against his waist. Oliver eyes now opened with joy. Moresee had washed away his despair.

"Is it OK for Moresee to join us in our bedroom?" Jules asked.

"Of course. He slept there every night with Mr. Jackson. Please follow me."

Hilda and Moresee followed Oliver. Jules couldn't stop looking over the bannister and imagining J. J. tumbling through the air to his death. The bannister was above Jules' stomach, almost to his chest. J. J. could not have accidentally fallen. Edwards and possibly Fitzgerald had thrown him over to his death. It hadn't been accidental. It had been intentional. They murdered J. J. But how to prove it? It was virtually impossible. Had they committed the perfect murder? Maybe he should forget the whole thing. Can't. Promises cannot be broken.

Oliver opened the door to J. J.'s bedroom. It was simple, clean, and beautifully furnished. The corners of the sheets were spread open to welcome the new occupants.

"Thank you, Oliver. This is quite lovely." Hilda nodded and smiled.

"You are at home." Oliver smiled. "Sleep well. When will you rise?"

"Early." Jules replied. "Around six."

After Oliver left, Hilda sighed, "We're safe here, but it's not our home."

"I'll take care of that tomorrow." Jules nodded in agreement. "It won't take too much time. We have the police backing us."

AFTER THE FUN

Jules rose early and happy. He wanted to take his morning run and try to sing "Oh What a Beautiful Morning." Unfortunately, he couldn't even hum a tune on key, and the morning run would be over until the huge pile of problems had been neatly put in place to make him stumble and fall. He brushed his teeth, shaved, showered, etc and told Hilda the bathroom was hers. Shortly after she entered, there was a knock on the bedroom door. Jules steeled himself. Now what? When he opened door, he was not surprised. He was shocked.

Oliver had a pushcart filled with covered food. "May I enter, Sir?"

"Hell yes! Good heavens! What a great surprise! Thank you, Oliver."

"My pleasure, sir." He put the food of a table. "Please ring when finished." He pointed to a cord hanging by the bed.

"Yes, of course," as if he had known of the cord, "and thanks from Hilda."

Oliver made a short bow, took the cart, and left.

Jules patiently waited for Hilda but had to peek beneath each shiny stainless lid. Under the small ones were choices of blueberries, strawberries, seedless grapes, cherries and melon slices. Under the larger lids were scrambled eggs with ham, bacon, or sausage and some buttered waffles. Jules wanted to

steal one piece of bacon, a cherry or something. He closed each lid quickly and his mouth watered as he waited. What's taking so long? My God, she's beautiful already. There's nothing she can do to be more beautiful. She's already there.

Hilda emerged fresh, smiling, and beautiful. She looked at the array of covered dishes and plates on the table.

"Oh, how wonderful!"

"I had to do something while you were getting ready. I hope I prepared the right things for you."

"Well, let me see." Hilda delicately peeked under each lid. "You did a sensational job, Oliver. Now that you know how and are so good at this, you may do it every morning when we get home. Now shall we eat and enjoy?"

And they did. When finished, Jules went over to bedside and pulled the cord. A few minutes later, Oliver knocked and entered.

"Did it suit your fancy?" Oliver asked.

"Perfectly." Jules replied. "Thank you for bringing it to us."

"My pleasure, Lady and Sir." Oliver took the cart of dishes and left.

"Do you need our car today, my dear?" Jules asked.

"No, why? What are you going to do?"

"I'm going to get our house problem solved. I'll check with the police captain first. He may have everything settled."

"That'll be just fine. Moresee and I will be waiting for you. He is so good and stays out our way so well that it's easy to forget he's here. I'll take him for a walk. Don't forget about your speech tomorrow night, my dear Senator."

Jules nodded but that thought was as distant as a star.

Jules drove down to the police station and asked for the chief. He wouldn't be in until tomorrow. He then decided to drive to their house. Maybe everything had been settled. When he arrived, it was obvious nothing had changed. Bars covered windows and doors and three guards had the house surrounded. Jules continued his ride to county headquarters.

When parked he didn't know exactly where to start or whom to contact. He walked to the front desk.

"I need to talk to someone about a house that's been condemned."

The nice young lady smiled, "Yes, sir, and what is your name, sir."

"Jules Cameron."

"Thank you, sir. Please sit down over there and someone will be with you momentarily."

Jules nodded. Things were going easily and well. He sat down and enjoyed looking around the mammoth interior that was akin to an ancient palace. His wait was only five or so minutes. Two armed guards arrived.

"Mr. Cameron?"

Jules thought of saying "no" and beating a hasty retreat, but he realized that wouldn't work. He nodded and asked,

"Yes, what's the problem?"

"No problem, sir. We're here to help you."

Oh my, he thought. Are they playing that game again? "Is the help regarding the status of our house?"

"Please come with us, sir. We won't let anything hurt you. I'll lead. You follow. Please do it peacefully. We don't want to use force."

"Thank you. How nice of you to help. Where am I?"

"All your questions will be answered shortly. Can you walk OK? Do you need help?"

"How considerate of you. I think I'm alright."

One guard walked ahead. The larger guard stayed close behind Jules. They took the elevator to the third floor, walked down a wide shinny clean hallway, past office after office, and finally came to a door they opened. There was no name on the office, only the number 3162.

"Cameron." The lead guard explained to the petite receptionist who wore huge black rimmed glasses that masked her small face.

Was she ashamed of her face or was she trying to look intellectual? Jules wondered.

"The door to your right. Dr. Gossart will be with you shortly." She glanced at Jules and returned to her paperwork,

OK, Jules thought, I'm a mental case again and didn't have his tapes to prove the set-up. When experts say you're nuts, how can you win? Let the games begin.

Dr. Gossart was tall and thin. His smile was warm and understanding as he approached Jules.

"Good-morning, Mr. Cameron. You're looking fit today."

"You also, good doctor."

"Thank you, Mr. Cameron. Please come over to this nice leather couch, and make yourself as comfortable as possible."

"How nice of you and how long should this take, doctor?"

"Not much time at all. We're here to help you. Why don't you tell me what seems to be bothering you today and any problems you might be having that we can solve for you."

"That's great! I came here, doctor, because our home has been impounded and has been boarded up so no one can get in or out. Also, three guards are there preventing entry. I came here to solve this problem."

"Is this true?" The doctor turned to the guards.

"Not at all, sir. There are no boards or guards around his house." The larger of the two replied and shook his head at the ridiculous remark.

"Wonderful!" Jules turned toward the door. "My problem has been miraculously solved. May I leave now?"

"Please, Mr. Cameron. When you rush things, they tend to get destroyed. This will just take a few moments. Just relax on the sofa. If you'd like to lie down and close your eyes, please do."

"Then I'll be able to leave?"

"Please relax and be patient. Now tell me about your house."

"As I said before, it has bars over the doors and windows and guards in front of all entryways to prevent entry by anyone."

"Is this so?" The doctor smiled as he again asked the guards.

"No, sir. There are no bars—no guards—no problems." The guard shook his head again and almost yawned.

"All right," Jules nodded in agreement, "hop in my car. It'll take fifteen minutes and you can see who is telling the truth."

"I'm not sure you should be allowed to drive." The doctor looked at Jules with sincere care.

"Then let's hop in your car and I'll lead the way."

"I am behind schedule already today. Perhaps tomorrow. Would you like some medicine or to close your eyes for a moment?"

"No, thank you, again Doctor, but I am confused. Maybe I've forgotten where I live. Maybe I'm completely lost. What is the address of my house?"

The smaller guard told the address.

"Could you write that down for me?" Jules asked. "I don't want to get lost again. Where am I now?"

The smaller guard wrote the address and handed it to Jules who nodded a thanks.

"And what does it look like?" Jules asked expectantly.

"It's a nice, secluded house on a knoll." The guard sounded friendly.

"And it's white, isn't it?" Jules continued.

"Right!" The shorter guard nodded vigorously.

"And it's a large house, and what is the color of the shutters?"

"Green." The short guard was happy to answer.

"And how many stories to my big house."

"Two." The guards were close to laughing. This was fun.

"Fine, Doctor. May I use my phone for a moment?"

"You still have your phone? They didn't take it immediately? Please hand me your phone."

Jules complied and then put his right hand on his back pocket.

"Keep your hands where we can see them." The big guard commanded.

Jules quietly pulled his tall wallet from his back right pocket and waved it in the air. "No harm." He smiled innocently.

When J. J. had decided to stop wearing suits, he had this long, expensive, leather wallet that he'd put in the inside pocket of his jacket. When he stopped wearing jackets, it was too large for his pants—period. Rather than throw it away he offered it to Jules who thought it was terrific and something he'd never buy for himself. He cheerfully took it and treasured it. Yes, it stuck out of his back pocket, but so what. It could shine proudly for all. Jules opened it slowly.

The guards kept their hands on their weapons as they watched. Jules faced them.

Jules pulled from the wallet a nine by eleven paper, refolded it, and put it back in the billfold. Opened another and did the same. The third one he opened he handed it to Dr. Gossart. It was a nine by eleven picture of his house. He then faced the two guards.

"What was the address of the house you saw?" Jules asked.

One of the guards gave the address. Jules turned to the doctor. The doctor saw the address in the photograph and nodded. Jules turned back to the guards.

"And what did you say is the color of the house?" He asked.

The larger one spoke confidently, "White."

"Very good," Jules nodded, "and the trim?"

The guard was getting suspicious. "Green." He reluctantly said.

"OK," Jules agreed, "and last question, how many stories is it?"

The two looked at each other, "Two." The smaller one spoke and tried to sound sure.

"Thank you, sirs." Jules nodded to them. "As you can see, Doctor Gossart, the house with the address they gave you is a grey stone house with grey trim the same shade as the stone. It is a one-story house. I think these guards need your help. May I leave now?"

Dr. Gossart's mouth stared angrily at Jules. "What the hell is going on? Are you playing games with me?" He handed the large photo of the house back to Jules who refolded it and tucked it back into his tall wallet.

"They are the ones playing the games." Jules replied. "They've never been to my house. They have never seen it. The photo tells the truth. They don't."

The Doctor turned to the guards. "What do you have to say for yourselves?"

"The picture is a fake." The smaller guard replied. "We were there. We know what we saw."

"And was the house boarded up with guards around it?"

"No, sir, Doctor. It's a white wood house with green trim. It is not impounded in any way. There are no guards or bars. He's lying. Don't let him go."

'Please, Dr. Gossart," Jules said quietly, "please call the police chief in Mill Valley, and he'll tell you the truth."

The two guards looked at each other wondering what to say or do as Dr. Gossart dialed and waited. As he hung up the phone, he turned to Jules, "The Captain is out today and won't be back until tomorrow."

"That's right," Jules agreed. "I forgot. Let's get in your car and drive out to my house and see who is and isn't telling the truth."

"As I told you earlier, I have a full schedule. This has taken more time than I expected or can afford. You'll have to stay overnight. We'll work it out tomorrow."

"This is amazing in America. I was taught early in school that in America you were innocent until proven guilty. Now you're telling me that I and my picture are lying. You believe words rather than evidence."

"You, Mr. Cameron, are questionable in many ways. You set out to trick us. You tried to make fools of these honorable guards. It was a clever trick, but it didn't work. Why should I trust you with your record more than county guards?"

"I understand, Doctor. Now tomorrow—if it turns out that everything I've said is correct and everything they said is wrong, what will be my reward and what will be their penalty. Will they lose their jobs or will they be your new patients? And should I sue for the cost of my time?"

The two guards stiffened. They did not like the direction.

Dr. Gossart faced the guards. "What do you have to say for yourselves?"

"Go there yourself, Doctor, tomorrow morning on your way here and you'll be able to see the truth with your own eyes."

Jules couldn't believe himself. They were going to remove the bars and guards immediately. HOORAY! He shouted to himself. He had won without going through a tremendous amount of paperwork and time.

Dr. Gossart donned a depreciating smile, "Why of course. I live in Mill Valley, too. I can drive by on my way here. It will only take minutes. What do you think is value of your time, Mr. Cameron?"

Jules nodded. He had to be careful. He didn't want to ruin his gain. The pictures of his house should be on the front pages of the newspapers –hopefully Oliver had complied. He couldn't take pictures of their house on the way home and e-mail it to the doctor because the doctor had his phone. He would trust Oliver.

"In regard to the value of my time, you are right, Doctor." Jules continued. "Presently it's pennies. However, I'm taking the late Mr. Jackson's place in his run for senator. I'm giving my acceptance speech tomorrow evening at the late Mr. Jackson's residence. Please attend, Doctor."

"You're running for Senator?" The doctor almost laughed.

"Yes, Doctor, I am. As I said, the present value of my time is zero, but if my initial speech is successful, the value should rise rapidly.

I'm sure I'll be able to find a hungry lawyer who will start the cost of the suit much, much higher than you can even imagine. I'll be rich and you'll have a lot of explaining to do. Do you want to lock me up or am I free to go?" He turned and looked at both guards, "I'm not asking for your names because I'll never and I mean never forget your faces. However, if I may go, I'll forget the suit and dismiss all the lies told to me today. May I leave now?"

"Please, Doctor Gossart, hold him until you see the house tomorrow morning." The large guard replied.

"I'll sue the both of you, also. It'll cost you your jobs and a lot more. You may all come to Jerry Jackson's house tomorrow evening to hear me. If you don't let me go now, tomorrow will be more than a nightmare for all of you."

The Doctor hesitated, looked at the guards whose faces looked pained, and said, "If what you say is a lie, you're the one in deep, deep trouble—understand? You may go, but don't do anything fancy like you did with another doctor."

"Thank you, Doctor. Would you please return my phone and give me your e-mail address? I'll send you Jerry Jackson's address and the scheduled time."

The doctor followed instructions and handed both to Jules. He then turned to the larger guard and asked, "Did you actually see his house?"

"We think so. It was what we were told. We were just following instructions. He's not supposed to leave. We're in deep trouble now."

The doctor put his hand on his forehead and said to Jules, "Get the hell out of here."

GUESTS

Jules stood by the window with Moresee sitting by the bed. The early April evening was becoming dark quickly. Jules was going to watch to see who was arriving, but it was too early. He walked over to the bed and sat by Moresee.

"Moresee, I don't know how to tell you this—I don't like your name. Now you've got to look at it this way—J. J., who gave you your name is gone. I'm the one who's stuck calling you 'Moresee' all the time. Since I am now your new boss, I'm going to change your name right now. You are no longer Moresee. You are now Morse—just Morse. I bless you with your new name Morse."

Jules lifted Moresee's head to look in his eyes. Moresee just blinked and wondered if something was wrong with his eyes. He was sure the problem would be fixed.

"Good! I'm glad you agree. You are now Morse."

Jules got off the bed, walked across the room toward the exit door and called in a stern voice,

"Morse, Morse come!"

Morse looked puzzled for a moment but rose and obeyed. Jules smiled broadly. He had finally won something. He led Morse back to the bed and they both sat. Jules rubbed Morse's head, back, and chest with loving care.

"I've got to tell you, Morse, everything's going to hell. I'm supposed to replace J. J. in the race for Senator. That's a joke. Your master had built a business and became rich and powerful. He was a great guy. They say I'm a lot like him. No way! I'm not like him in any way. We're opposites. He was great. I'm a bum.

"I've done nothing, Morse, nothing. Not only am I a bum but to top it off I'm a Republican. Republicans are an expensive joke in California. They spend a lot of money to get elected and after losing as usual and expected, everyone laughs at their ignorant stupidity. I have no chance of winning. Everyone knows that. It's an expensive joke and I've got no money. I'm supposed to give a speech tonight to convince all the laughers in California to vote for me.

"All I've wanted to do, Morse, is find out who murdered your wonderful owner. You, Morse, showed me who it is. Thank you. You're terrific. You did easily and quickly that I could not do pushing my mind hard as hell.

"OK, now we both know the killer. He and his boss will probably be here tonight. I'll have to keep you up here so you can't attack him again. But what the hell can I do about it? Because of you, Morse, I know the killer. He and his boss will be here. I'm sure of that. If I point that out to the crowd, they'll be delighted and sue the hell out of me. Since I'm broke now, I'll probably end up in jail.

"That's right, I am broke, Morse. You've gone from being rich to being poor. The wonderful thing about you is that you'll love me regardless. Of course, so will my wife, Hilda and my soon to be baby will be stuck in my mess. I'm lucky to have you three. Now, somehow I've got to pull myself out of this mess."

Jules heard a car door close gently and politely. He gave a nudge to Morse's collar and they both went to the window. Morse sat down beside him. The other door opened and closed politely.

"Oh, for God's sake, Morse! Look who's the first one here—Alex, and look who's holding his arm as if he were an valuable possession—Linda. She's in charge, Morse. She owns him. Alex doesn't know it yet, but he will. I'm sure Alex came early to come up here to talk to me. I wonder what about. Maybe he does know Linda owns him. Could he be thinking marriage? Hell no! Not Alex. But maybe, Morse, maybe. Interesting. He won't get up here. Our darling, Hilda, is guarding the staircase. No one will be coming up. We'll find out later.

"Here come more cars, Morse. Here they come. The two assassins came about an hour ago. J. J. had three covering him, and he was considered unimportant. I've got two covering me. I guess I'm a joke. I hope I put them to sleep, Morse. That would be the best news coverage they could give me—fictional or from their twisted minds of hate.

A series of doors opened and slammed shut.

"Oh, damn, Morse, here comes an interesting group. It's Mr. Floss and four guys following him. They must be from his detective company. They look pretty big and powerful. Why did he bring four big guys with him?

"The car behind Floss must be Charlie's. A big Muslim robbed guy got out, jumped back into the car, they turned around and drove off. Charlie didn't want to be seen here with me. He didn't want Floss to make the connection. Floss saw him, and is staring at Charlie's car as it's leaving. This going to be interesting, Morse. Our enemies are arriving and staying. Our friends are leaving.

"Oh, Morse, speaking of enemies, here comes Dolph and his gang of three. He's the one who fired me, Morse. He wouldn't give me a couple of weeks leave to clear my mind about J. J.'s death. He took the opportunity to get rid of me. Angela is dressed nicely. She has a great figure. She's moving as if nervous and uncertain. The accountant, John Peter, is moving stiffly as if worried and big Ray is moving as if ready to go into battle.

"Guess who's coming now, Morse? You'll never guess so I'll tell you—it's my two head guys—my phycologists Dr. Stoulk and Dr. Gossart. And guess what? They're bringing an extra four guys with them. They're out to get me.

"Right next to them is Senator Hazelton and his two bodyguards. Oh, but look who's getting out of the car with them—the Rangers, murderer John Edwards and his boss, Tom Fitzgerald. But where was the driver, Pete Jonas? They didn't need a driver, dumbo Jules. They rode in the Senator's big limousine.

"You know what, Morse, old pal? There's a bunch of people waiting for me. Let's see, out of all below I have two friends, Hilda and Alex. Maybe Linda will back Alex but not me necessarily. When Oscar comes in from arranging the parking, he might back me. Where is Paul? What difference does it make? He wouldn't back me for sure.

"So, Morse old buddy, everyone else down there wants to destroy me one way or another. I wish I could bring you down with me. I know you'd try to protect me like you must have to tried to protect your dear J. J. But you must stay here. You'll be safe. Somehow I'll try to survive. Hope to see you in a little bit my new and wonderful pal Morse."

With that Jules rubbed Morse's back, lifted his chin, gave him a short kiss on the top of his head, and opened the bedroom door and headed down the circular staircase.

CALAMITY

Waiting for him at the bottom of the stairs was his beautiful Hilda. He gave her a short kiss on her left cheek and said,

"I've changed his name. He's no longer Moresee. He is now Morse. What do you think of that?"

Hilda's shook her head as if trying to waken. "Really? Amazing, truly amazing! It's not at all what I expected."

"Come on! Let's face our hangmen and get it done one way or another."

Hilda was still confused but followed and stayed close to Jules. She sensed something was seriously wrong and she stood by to help and protect. They walked across the foyer to the living room doors and were about to open them when Oliver came in the front door and rushed to open the doors for them.

Well, Jules thought, Oliver might be one more friend. Jules and Hilda walked into the living room. They were greeted with dead silence. Alex gave a couple of claps. Linda put her right hand over his and stopped the clapping.

Jules smiled. No one was sitting in the neatly assembled rows of steel portable chairs. All were standing. Conversation stopped as Jules and Hilda walked toward the fireplace. They grudgingly made a path for them. Jules got Alex's eyes and with a nod of his head motioned for him to join them. The group didn't make way for Alex and Linda. They pushed their way through.

Jules took a big step to get on the raised fireplace and helped Hilda to make the high step easier. Jules nodded for Alex to join him and he did with Linda.

"Ready for some action?" Jules whispered.

Alex nodded with a smile.

"Who can't you take?"

"No problem." Alex assured.

"Get Linda behind you against the fireplace. I'll do the same with Hilda. They can only attack us from the front and only a couple at a time can do it."

"They're dead." Alex raised his thumb and smiled.

Jules then turned and faced his enemies. Dolph and his gang of three were to his far left in front of the piano. Dolph covered a good portion of it. Slim Angela stood next to Dolph, then John Peter, and big Ray. The Floss group was the next and they looked ready to attack. In the middle were Dr. Stoulk and Dr. Gossart with their aides and then came the two Rangers with their gang.

Jules had to wonder which ones were fighters and which were lawyers who want to kill him legally and financially. The fighters could only climb up the fireplace two max at a time. He and Alex could handle that. Jules looked at each person for at least a minute before he started.

"Good-evening all. Please excuse the lack of snacks and drinks. This is not a celebration. I am here in quest of becoming Senator of the United States because Jerry Jackson, who would have been elected, was murdered and is no longer here.

"Mr. Jackson, or J. J., as he preferred to be called, was murdered just a few weeks ago. He was a remarkable man. Look at the beauty of this house and the landscape that surrounds it. It is a reflection of J. J. Everything J. J. did was clean and beautiful.

"He started a cutting tool distributorship with his good friend, Dolph Briskie. With J. J.'s money and guidance, the business grew and grew until a rival national company wanted it and paid high dollars to gain owner-ship. J. J. was set financially for life and decided to pursue a new career—that of guiding our country to make it as successful as he had made his company. His sudden and unexpected death changed everything.

"The Party he represented had a sure winner with J. J. He was strong, honorable, hardworking, and all he built was a reflection of these qualities. He would have been a superior senator. Now he is gone and a replacement is needed. I got the call and accepted. That is the reason I'm now standing in front of you. Now let me tell you of what I'll bring to you.

"I am a nobody. I have no idea who my mother or my father were. I was raised in multiple households and passed around like a bag of dirty clothes. No one wanted me for very long." Jules looked at the two psychologists, Dr. Stoulk and Dr. Gossart. They both frowned at him. Jules smiled back.

"I did well in high school and got good grades. When I was graduated, I had no desire or inclination to go to college. I didn't want to be a professional anything that required a college degree which in turn would bury me in debt. In fact, I had no desire to get a steady job and be stuck with an eight to five or whatever work regime. I didn't want to work. I wanted to make money with as little effort as possible, keep as much for myself as possible, and pay as little taxes on it as possible. My thought was, why should the government be rewarded for my work? If I did the work, I should get the money. How is that possible? Simple. Get a job in crime."

Jules looked at the Rangers and friends.

"I did. I started a business selling drugs. No, I didn't take drugs into my body. I sold them to the world of fools. Yes, I started making good money. I hid my actual earnings and paid the government as little as possible.

"At times, I even got money back from the government. That was great. I loved that. I had won and the government had lost. I had tricked them using their own laws, rules and regulations."

All in the assembled group were staring at him. Where the hell was this going? Hilda was also worrying.

"So what have I accomplished in my life? Just a few wonderful and remarkable things. J. J. took my hand, gave me a job in his company which made it possible for my wonderful wife, Hilda to marry me. She would not even date me as a criminal. J. J. became the father I never had. He guided me as to what was right or wrong. He tried to convert me from a bum to a man with honor.

"Now J. J. has been murdered and I know exactly who murdered him and how it was done." Jules fixed his eyes on Ranger John Edwards.

John Edwards stepped forward furiously. "Why the hell are you looking at me? Are you accusing me of murder?"

"I'm just looking at you, Ranger Edwards. I don't think that's a crime."

"It's a strong insinuation." One of the guys with the Rangers replied.

Must be a lawyer, Jules thought. "I only directed my eyes toward you. You seem to have a guilty conscience."

Ranger Edwards stepped forward in a hostile manner. The lawyer quickly restrained him.

Dr. Stoulk and Dr. Gossart stepped forward and turned to the assembly. "Please all of you, please be patient and understanding."Dr. Stoulk said in his most sympathetic voice. "When someone is seriously ill, you can't attack them. You must do your best to help." He then turned to face Jules. "Please, Mr. Cameron, please come down so we can help and repair you. It will be simple and all pain will be replaced by the return of good health. Please come down and join us, your friends."

"Thank you, Doctor Gossart." Jules replied. "I'm surprised at the amount of friends I have. Most of my friends I've never seen before or my failed memory can't remember them. Please tell me who you are and why you're here."

Doctors Stould and Gossart looked at each other. Dr. Gossart nodded and turned to Dolph's group. "Please tell Mr. Cameron why you are here."

Dolph moved his building of a body forward one step. "Cameron was always a problem in our business. J. J. was patient and tried to make Cameron a responsible employee. I think the failure of J. J.'s hard work and the persistent hostile attitude of Cameron led to J. J.'s death. Mr. Jackson did everything in his power to make Cameron a good employee. Much to Mr. Jackson's dismay, it never happened. Cameron remained a nail stuck between his ribs and close to his heart. I am sure this is why J. J. fell over the bannister accidentally or jumped over it in an intentional suicide to his death. In essence, Cameron killed the one person who was doing all in his power to help him. I am here hoping to see Cameron brought to the justice he deserves—prison or the death sentence he deserves."

Dolph took his miniature step backward to show he was finished.

"Mr. Floss," Dr. Gossart turned to the next group, "tell us your reason to attend this meeting."

"With pleasure." Floss stepped forward and looked directly at Jules. "We were hired by the most honorable and respected people in our country to protect Mr. Cameron from doing more harm to anyone or himself, and to especially protect his lovely wife, Hilda, from any harm from him."

"That is an absolute lie!" Hilda stepped forward in front of Jules and stood in front of him as if a shield. "Jules Cameron is no danger to anyone. He is kind, thoughtful, truthful, and the most intelligent person in this room. For any of you to attack his mental well-being is sick. You are the sick ones—not Jules. Get over it and get out of here!"

Jules had never seen her so furious.

"It is not a lie, lady," Floss shot back with equal fury, "Your husband is a serious problem to himself, to you and your soon to be baby, and to the rest of the world. He is sick. He needs to be cured. I even wonder if at times he dresses and acts like a Muslim. He's sick, lady. He needs to be cured." Floss then took his step backward.

Hilda stayed in front of Jules. Jules smiled and put his hands on her hips.

"Rangers," Dr. Gossart turned to the two with their associates, "do you have anything you'd like to say?"

"I sure do," Tom Fitzgerald, the boss, took the step forward, "if Mr. Jackson did not fall accidentally over the bannister or did not choose to commit suicide by jumping over it to his death, then Jules Cameron murdered him. There is no other possible explanation. This sick Cameron guy is so mentally deranged he knows he murdered his benefactor and his guilt is so great in his sick mind that he's trying to place Mr. Jackson's murder on anyone else. He is so sick he even looked at us as if we committed the crime. It is incredible. It is impossible. It shows how sick and need of repair Jules Cameron is. He needs your help, doctors. He is a danger to the world." He then took his step backward.

Jules turned to Alex and Linda. "I guess it's safe, old pal. Thanks for your backing. You two get going." He turned Hilda's head. "You get going, too."

"Never! I'm with you. This is terrible. I can't let it happen."

"Please, my dear wife." Jules gave her a kiss on her left cheek. "Don't worry. I've beaten them in the past. I'll do it again."

"I'm staying with you. Whatever they try to do to you, they'll have to do to me also. I'm with you."

Jules pulled her beside him and kept his arm around her waist. "Well, dear friends and gentlemen, what do you want me to do?"

"Come on down, my dear Jules," Dr. Stoulk gave his kindest and sweetest tone. "We want to help you."

"OK." Jules nodded and stepped off the mantle, turned, and lifted Hilda to the main floor.

Two men quickly pushed Hilda aside with a force that knocked her back to the mantle where she was flattened against it and used her arms to stand again.

"What the hell are you doing?" Jules yelled. "You can't treat my wife like that!"

"Cuff him," Dr. Stoulk order. It just took a couple of seconds for Jules' arms to be put behind his back and the cuffs applied. "Bring him to my car."

As they started walking toward the large doors of the living room, the doors swung open and the Chief of Police and four policemen entered. The Chief stopped his men and looked at the two Rangers.

"Rangers John Edwards and Tom Fitzgerald, you are under arrest for the murder of Jerry Jackson. Raise your hands and stand completely still."

"You've made a grave mistake." Ranger Fitzgerald said quickly. "Here is the problem. We've caught him for you."

"Take his cuffs off and put cuffs on these two he ordered his men. "Jules Cameron is the hero. He solved this case. You two murdered Jerry Jackson. It will be an easy case. Jules Cameron solved it. He did a magnificent job."

The police left with the two Rangers in tow. All the rest looked at Jules who was tight with Hilda. They were in shock. What the hell was going on?

♦♦♦

After all had left, Jules shook his head and kissed Hilda on her lips. Alex and Linda were still there. Oliver was standing in the back of the living room as if part of the furniture. All others had left.

"What the hell happened?" Alex asked.

"Damned it I know." Jules shook his head in bewilderment. "Do me a favor, please. Thank you for standing by me. You're a true friend. Please leave and take Linda with you."

"Not yet. We have to know how you did this." Alex replied, and Linda nodded.

"I don't know." Jules shook his head and smiled.

The living room doors opened and Paul walked into the room. He ignored Alex, Linda, and even Hilda and walked straight to Jules.

"You owe me one and a half million bucks." He put his face just a few inches from Jules'.

"OK, but what the hell for?"

"The Ranger's driver, Pete whatever, has tapes of the guys conversation after they threw my brother over the rail to his death. He gave me the tapes for one and a half million bucks and he'll testify to all he heard in the car afterwards. The police have the tapes and Pete safely in custody. I told the police it was all your idea. I don't want to be involved in any way. It cost me one and a half million bucks to buy Pete what's his name. You are getting all the credit. I get none. All I want from you is my million and a half."

"I don't have a damn cent. I'm broke."

"Oh, that's right. You missed the reading of the will yesterday. Yeah, yeah, you were here and so didn't get your mail. Oliver was left five percent of J. J.'s fortune. You were left twenty percent which will be over seventy million bucks and the rest goes to me. Now I have two favors to ask of you—give me my one and a half million bucks and get the hell out of my life!"

The next day the headlines blared—

PERFECT CRIME SOLVED BY AMATEUR SLEUTH

THE END

www.ingramcontent.com/pod-product-compliance
Lightning Source LLC
Chambersburg PA
CBHW020523120726
47904CB00003B/951